FAR-FLUNG ADVENTURES

# Corby Flood

## ALSO BY PAUL STEWART & CHRIS RIDDELL

### FAR-FLUNG ADVENTURES
*Fergus Crane*
*Hugo Pepper*

### THE EDGE CHRONICLES

#### THE TWIG TRILOGY
*Beyond the Deepwoods*
*Stormchaser*
*Midnight over Sanctaphrax*

#### THE QUINT TRILOGY
*The Curse of the Gloamglozer*
*The Winter Knights*
*Clash of the Sky Galleons*

#### THE ROOK TRILOGY
*The Last of the Sky Pirates*
*Vox*
*Freeglader*

*The Immortals*

### THE BARNABY GRIMES SERIES
*Curse of the Night Wolf*
*Return of the Emerald Skull*
*Legion of the Dead*
*Phantom of Blood Alley*

FAR-FLUNG ADVENTURES

# Corby Flood

## Paul Stewart & Chris Riddell

A YEARLING BOOK

Text, illustrations, and cover art copyright © 2005 by Paul Stewart and Chris Riddell

All rights reserved. Published in the United States by Yearling, an imprint of Random House Children's Books, a division of Random House, Inc., New York. Originally published in hardcover in Great Britain by Doubleday, an imprint of Random House Children's Books, a division of the Random House Group Ltd., London, in 2005, and subsequently published in hardcover in the United States by David Fickling Books, an imprint of Random House Children's Books, New York, in 2006.

Yearling and the jumping horse design are registered trademarks of Random House, Inc.

Visit us on the Web! www.randomhouse.com/kids

Educators and librarians, for a variety of teaching tools, visit us at www.randomhouse.com/teachers

The Library of Congress has cataloged the hardcover edition of this work as follows:
Stewart, Paul.
Corby Flood / by Paul Stewart & Chris Riddell.
    p.   cm. — (Far-flung adventures)
Summary: While traveling with her family aboard the S.S. *Euphonia,* eight-year-old Corby Flood accidentally attracts the murderous attentions of five men, clad in bowler hats, called the Brotherhood of Clowns as she investigates the mysterious singing coming from the ship's hold.
ISBN 978-0-385-75090-5 (trade) — ISBN 978-0-385-75091-2 (lib. bdg.) —
ISBN 978-0-307-49541-9 (ebook)
[1. Ocean travel—Fiction. 2. Clowns—Fiction. 3. Ships—Fiction.] I. Riddell, Chris. II. Title.
PZ7.S84975Cor 2006
[Fic]—dc22
2005031865

ISBN 978-0-385-75097-4 (pbk.)

Printed in the United States of America
10 9 8 7 6 5 4 3 2 1

First Yearling Edition 2012

Random House Children's Books supports the First Amendment and celebrates the right to read.

For Julie – P.S.
For my mother-in-law, Ann – C.R.

THE BEGUM OF DANDOON

DORALAKIA

ISSARI

THE WHEEZING DONKEY

THE LAUGHING GOAT

THE COAST OF DALCRETIA

THE DANCING PIG

THE COUNTING OX

# 1. The Saddest Song

I t's quiet and dark here, and the forest floor sways and rolls beneath my feet. Sometimes I stumble, but I do not fall over, because I'm trapped inside this tree where it is always dark. Oh, how I long to see the sun again.

How did I get here? I can hardly remember . . .

Ah, yes, that's it. I followed my tongue. The sweet petals tasted so good, melting in my mouth, until I walked into this tree and got trapped inside.

Now there is no more sun. Just quiet and darkness and swaying. I feel so sad. My heart is so full of sadness that it must surely break . . .

I will sing to let the sadness out. Perhaps if I sing, the forest will stop rolling and swaying, and the sun will come back, and my heart will not break . . . just yet.

The S.S. *Euphonia*, ablaze with twinkling lights, glided across a moonlit sea. Its funnels were topped with streams of frothy white smoke, its gleaming sides peppered with brightly lit portholes and its decks thronged with glamorous promenaders, taking the air and watching the stars.

It was all so wonderful. So magical . . .

Corby Flood reached up and touched the glass that protected the faded poster. She traced the lettering in the starry sky above the beautiful ship with a finger.

'The S.S. Euphonia,' she read. '*"Empress of the Seas". Enjoy the voyage of a lifetime aboard this miracle of modern nautical engineering! Cruise the oceans of the world and explore the magical places along the way! Book now for the deluxe ten-ports-of-call cruise and receive your free copy of the famous* Hoffendinck's Guide.'

Corby's grip tightened on the battered leather-bound book she was clutching under her arm.

'Why, if it isn't one of those *Hoffendinck's Guides*,' said a gloomy voice.

Corby turned to find Captain Boris Belvedere standing before her. The captain – never cheerful at the best of

2

times – was looking gloomier than ever. With his sagging skin and drooping moustache, he looked like nothing so much as a disappointed walrus.

'Didn't think we had any of those left on board,' he said. 'After all, it's not as if the poor old *Euphonia* stops anywhere interesting any more. In fact she doesn't stop anywhere at all any more! Dandoon to Harbour Heights non-stop, and back again . . .' His voice was low, lugubrious and tinged with regret. 'More's the pity.' He sighed. 'Hauling cargo is all the old "Empress of the Seas" and I are fit for. That, and the odd passenger or two who can't afford anything better . . .' He looked Corby up and down somewhat disapprovingly.

'Well, I think she's a lovely ship,' said Corby. 'And after Father's great disappointment . . .' Her voice wavered for a moment and she swallowed hard. 'Mother says we've got to learn to make the best of things and try to stay cheerful.' And she gave the captain what she hoped was a meaningful stare.

'Yes, well, ahem . . .' The captain turned away. 'Sometimes that's easier said than done, little girl. Especially when the bilge pump has broken and your first *and* your second engineers have left for better jobs.'

He cast a gloomy eye over the chipped paintwork, rusty railings and scuffed decking of the old ship.

'Still, that's only to be expected when hardly anything works any more,' he went on. 'The automatic parasols, the self-adjusting railings, the moving windbreaks . . .' He gestured about him in a wide arc. 'The *Euphonia*'s only fit for the scrapheap,' he muttered, shaking his head. 'Just like me!'

'Good news, Captain,' came a smooth, polished voice, and both he and Corby turned to see the ship's first officer Lieutenant Jon-Jolyon Letchworth-Crisp standing there, a suave smile on his lips. 'Arthur's managed to fix the bilge pump,' he said. 'At least, for the time being . . .'

JON-JOLYON LETCHWORTH-CRISP

'Good news?' said Captain Belvedere. 'If you say so, Letchworth-Crisp, if you say so . . .' The captain turned and walked slowly away. 'I'll be in my cabin if you need me,' he added gloomily. 'Though why anybody should need me, I don't know . . .'

Jon-Jolyon turned to Corby and flashed a brittle smile. 'And how is young Miss Corby Flood today?' he asked.

'Fine, thanks,' said Corby.

'And your delightful mother and father?'

6

'Also fine.'

'And your four energetic brothers?'

Corby nodded. They both knew that there was only one person in the Flood family he was truly interested in. 'The same as ever,' she said. 'And before you ask, so is my *enchanting older sister, Serena.*'

Jon-Jolyon grinned. 'Glad to hear it. Do give her my very best regards, won't you?' he said, as he turned on his heels and strode off. 'And I hope we shall all meet up at dinner,' he called back over his shoulder.

Corby smiled – a smile which faded the moment she was sure the lieutenant had gone. She opened *Hoffendinck's Guide* and, taking the pencil that dangled on a piece of string around her neck, she started writing . . .

# THE HERMIT ISLANDS

These tiny crags, several hundred in number, were occupied by hermit fishermen for many years and are ideal for an afternoon picnic if passing. Consult the captain for details of tides, and always have a stout rowing boat at the ready in case of emergencies.

Some of the more interesting islands are:

*Mortimer's Crag* – very rocky, but home to a legendary mermaid so hideous that she is said to frighten fishermen to death with one look.

*Stefan's Pile* – covered in soft, grey sea-moss up to five feet thick, and home to eider crabs.

*The Old Man of Fub* – famous for its nesting colony of blue-tailed goobies. Well worth a visit.

OLD SUSANNE

## SIGHTS TO LOOK OUT FOR:

*De Witt's Moonlight Flying Fish*; *a.k.a. Love Fish* – on moonlit nights, these extraordinary fish can be seen swimming in large shoals close to the surface of the ocean. As the moonlight glints on the tops of the waves, the love fish engage in elaborate displays, leaping into the air in graceful arcs.

Legend has it that any who witness the flight of the love fish fall instantly in love.

# NOTES

Lieutenant Jon-Jolyon Letchworth-Crisp

| Good points | Bad points |
|---|---|
| nice manners | bites his ginger nails |
| Smiles a lot | Smiles a lot |
| good looking (sort of if you like that sort of thing) | a bit smarmy |
| | Too much hair grease |
| always asks how you are | doesn't listen to your answers |
| uniform is very neat. | |
| | only interested in Serena |
| | Always trying to impress her with stories of how good and clever and brilliant at things he is. |

Corby stopped writing for a moment and gazed reflectively out to sea. How strange, she thought, to be writing notes about the people she met on board, instead of notes about the interesting places mentioned in *Hoffendinck's Guide.*

When they boarded the S.S. *Euphonia,* she'd been so excited by the prospect of all the fascinating sights she would see on her voyage home to Harbour Heights – not that Corby could call Harbour Heights 'home' exactly. The only home she had ever known was the large white bungalow in Dandoon where she had been born eight years earlier. And as for the sights, it wasn't long before Corby had discovered that the closest she would ever get was peering at them on the distant horizon as the ship sailed past.

Still, at least she could read all about them in the guide. She squinted at a tiny black speck on the horizon.

Was that Mortimer's Crag? she wondered. Or Stefan's Pile? But she was too far away even to make a guess, she realized with a sigh.

At that moment Corby heard the sound of low

muttering and shuffling footsteps coming up the stairs from the cabins below her.

Uh-oh, she thought, snapping shut *Hoffendinck's Guide*. It's the Hattenswillers!

Mr and Mrs Hattenswiller appeared at the top of the stairs. They were both wearing tall, conical hats with ear flaps, and matching ankle-length coats with lots of pockets. Whenever she met them, Mr Hattenswiller would click his heels together and nod at Corby politely, while Mrs Hattenswiller would smile, and the pair of them never failed to exchange greetings. And that was where the problem lay – for no matter how hard she listened, Corby could never, ever, make out what they were saying.

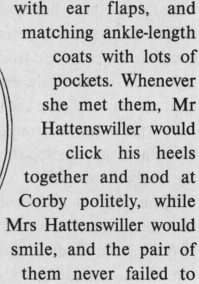

MR.& MRS. HATTENSWILLER

Sometimes *Mr* Hattenswiller would speak, and his wife would smile knowingly as though he had just said the cleverest thing. But Corby had heard only a mumbled murmur. And sometimes *Mrs* Hattenswiller would say something, and her husband would nod vigorously in agreement. But again, Corby had heard nothing but a quiet whisper.

Once, taking a chance, she'd replied that she was 'very well, thank you' – but both Hattenswillers had looked at her as if she were mad. His eyebrows had shot upwards, her smile had frozen, and the pair of them had continued on their way, exchanging puzzled comments that, of course, Corby couldn't hear properly.

No, far better all round if she avoided them, she thought, as she scooted through the side door and onto the starboard deck.

It was warm outside, with the sun shining down out of a cloudless sky. It was also very bright – particularly after the shadowy darkness of the hallway at the top of the stairs. Corby screwed up her eyes and stepped blindly ahead, only to trip over something in her path.

It was a leg, or rather, a pair of legs belonging to the man from Cabin 21. He was sitting in a deckchair wearing dark glasses, a white suit and navy-blue deck shoes. The man from Cabin 21 always wore dark glasses, a white suit and navy-blue deck shoes, and he sat in the same mechanical deckchair on the same deck every day – when he wasn't in Cabin 21, that is.

'Sorry,' Corby called across to him politely – even though she didn't think it was her fault at all; even though, if the truth be told, she thought it was the man from Cabin 21 who should have apologized to *her*.

THE MAN FROM CABIN 21

But he neither apologized nor acknowledged Corby's apology. It was impossible to know whether he'd heard her – or if he even realized what had happened. That was the thing about the man from Cabin 21. He sat all day every day in his deckchair on the starboard deck, staring out to sea – and most of the time no one knew whether he was looking for land, or just at the waves, or was fast asleep.

Trust her, Corby thought, to avoid the Hattenswillers, only to fall over the man from Cabin 21. Shaking her head, she continued along the starboard walkway, past the raised main deck, the funnels, the lifeboats, more stairs and on towards the prow of the ship.

This was where the really grand cabins used to be – the ones with the big bathrooms and huge sitting rooms and bedrooms the size of ballrooms. Cabin 21 was the only grand cabin left. The others had all been knocked through to make room for an enormous cargo hold.

Corby arrived at the prow, which was – as always – deserted. That was why she liked it.

The Hattenswillers seldom ventured far from their cabin; nor did the man from Cabin 21. As for her family, they were always far too preoccupied with other things to spend time taking in the view. That left the five sinister gentlemen in their smart suits and bottle-green hats, who had made such a fuss over the loading of their luggage when they'd boarded the S.S. *Euphonia* in Dandoon. Not only did they keep themselves to themselves, but they always stopped talking whenever Corby, or anyone else, passed by.

But Corby loved the prow of the ship, especially standing up at the very front, with the wind in her hair and the sun in her eyes, watching the sharp, jutting prow slice through the oncoming turquoise-blue waves. It was, she thought, like the blade of a knife cutting through a never-ending piece of rippling silk in an absolutely straight line.

Suddenly, from behind her, above the rumble of the engines and the splashing of the waves, she heard another sound. It was a long, sad cry - mournful, yet curiously tuneful. At first Corby thought it was seagulls, but the ship was too far out at sea for any of them to be close by - and neither was it the wind whistling through the ropes . . .

Leaving the prow, Corby stepped forwards a little way and stopped. She cocked her head to one side.

The sound seemed to be coming from the port side. She took another step, paused and listened again. No, the starboard side, she thought, retracing her steps . . .

Or was it the port side, after all?

The next moment she realized that either side would do, for the curious sound was coming from the staircase in between them - the staircase at the front of the ship which led down to the hold. Standing on the top stair, Corby listened intently, her head tilted and her brow furrowed with concentration.

The strange, mournful cry rose and fell, now high and wavering, now low and haunting. Rising and falling, rising and falling . . . It was as if a sad wolf was singing to the moon, or a lonely songbird was calling to its mate.

It was the saddest song Corby had ever heard.

She would have liked to go down to investigate, but the doors to the hold, which had CABINS 22-40 written on them, were locked, and only Captain Belvedere had the key. Besides, just then, in the distance, the gong for dinner sounded.

# 2. The Empress of the Seas

**W**hat was that? It sounded like the palace cymbal, only more distant.

When the palace cymbal sounds, the little girl comes with the fresh, sweet meadow grass and honey flowers. But I know it cannot be the palace cymbal because the little girl doesn't come. Not any more . . .

I am stuck, trapped in this hollow tree, and the little girl never comes now, only the strange man with the green head and creaking feet. The water he gives me is stale, but the sweet white petals are good . . .

But he hasn't been for so long, and I am hungry, and thirsty . . . and sad.

'What's keeping Arthur?' said Captain Belvedere gloomily, his fingers drumming on the worn white tablecloth in front of him.

'I'll go and see, sir,' said Lieutenant Letchworth-Crisp smoothly. He stood up and bowed his glistening head. 'Ladies, if you'll excuse me . . .'

'Yes, yes, of course,' said Mrs Flood with a bright smile. She turned to her eldest daughter as the lieutenant left the small dining room. 'Such a polite young man, don't you think, Serena? Though a little less hair-oil might be an improvement . . .'

Corby giggled, and Serena shot her a withering look before turning to her mother. 'Mother, please!' she whispered, flushing a delicate shade of pink. 'You're embarrassing me.'

They were all sitting at one of three circular dining-room tables. At the centre of each table

20

was a large silver cover, which was connected to the
ceiling above by a snaking silver pipe. A few moments
later, the sound of Lieutenant Letchworth-Crisp's
voice could plainly be heard from somewhere below
them.

'I don't care if you were mending the bilge
pump, Arthur!' he was shouting. 'The
captain wants his dinner! And so, for
that matter, do I!'

Corby got out her copy of
*Hoffendinck's Guide* and opened it . . .

which is just as well, because it is not recommended on a full stomach.

# LONESOME SKERRY

This island is famous for being home to Captain Lemuel Gibbons, whose ship, the *Bonnie Rose*, ran aground here two hundred years ago.

Although his crew was rescued, Captain Gibbons refused to leave his beloved ship, and remained on the island for twenty-five years, attempting to repair it. He survived on a diet of spitting whelks, and by taking in laundry from passing ships in return for snuff and sherry.

The phrases 'as crisp as a Gibbons shirt' and 'a Lemuel sneeze on washday' originated here.

## SIGHTS TO LOOK OUT FOR:

*Spitting Whelks (buccinum sputis)*, which on occasions, and for no apparent reason, spurt a pale green liquid, are found only on Lonesome Skerry.

*The Wreck of the Bonnie Rose* – off the south-east coast, now no more than a few whelk-encrusted timbers sticking out of the waves.

*Captain Lemuel Gibbons' Treehouse* – at the top of a skerry pine, should only be visited by experienced tree-climbers with a head for heights.

*Washday Cove* – sandy beach on the north of the island, where

# NOTES

The dining Room S.S.Euphonia

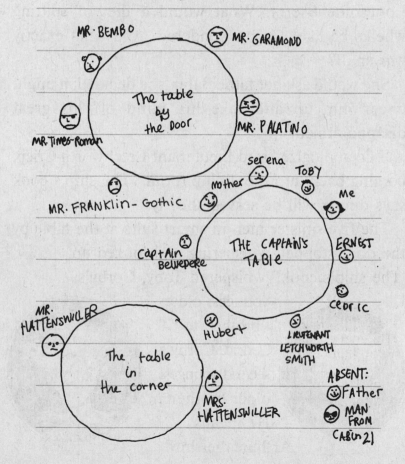

MR·BEMBO

MR·GARAMOND

The table by the Door

MR·Times-Roman

MR·PALATINO

MR·FRANKLIN- Gothic

serena

Mother

TOBY

Me

Captain Belvedere

THE CAPTAIN'S TABLE

ERNEST

CEDRIC

MR· HATTENSWILLER

Hubert

LIEUTENANT LETCHWORTH SMITH

The table in the corner

MRS. HATTENSWILLER

ABSENT:
☺ FAther
😠 MAN FROM
CABIN 21

Corby finished drawing the sunglasses on the man from Cabin 21 and paused. Her eyes wandered across to the opposite page of the guide.

Out there, somewhere across the sea, was Lonesome Skerry. What would a diet of spitting whelks be like? Corby wondered. And what exactly *was* snuff?

She would ask her father later, she decided; it might cheer him up and take his mind off his great disappointment . . .

'I do apologize,' said Lieutenant Letchworth-Crisp, coming back into the dining room. 'The ship's cook says dinner will be served shortly.'

The five sinister men in smart suits at the table by the door stopped whispering and looked up. 'The ship's cook!' whispered Toby, Corby's

youngest older brother, to Cedric, Corby's second youngest older brother. 'He means Arthur, the third

engineer!' Corby's four brothers sniggered.

'Settle down, boys,' said Mrs Flood sternly. Serena smiled at the lieutenant as he sat down at their table. 'That's quite all right, Jon-Jolyon,' she said sweetly, and nudged Corby with her elbow. 'Put that book away,' she whispered out of the corner of her mouth.

HUBERT

ERNEST

Corby closed the book as Captain Belvedere leaned over, a faraway look in his eyes.

'Still got your *Hoffendinck's Guide*, I see,' he said in his gloomy voice. 'Must be the last copy left on board.'

'It is,' said Letchworth-Crisp suavely. 'I found it stuffed behind the steam press in the old purser's office. Thought the little girl might find it amusing.' He flashed a winning smile at Serena.

Corby frowned. In fact, she'd seen him about to throw it overboard in a fit of temper on the first day of the voyage. She'd practically had to beg him not to – and had then had to listen to him moaning on about how he was a lieutenant and not a skivvy, and why couldn't Arthur clean out the purser's office?

'Takes me back to the old days,' said Captain Belvedere, 'when the S.S. *Euphonia* really *was* the Empress of the Seas . . .'

'Here we go,' muttered Letchworth-Crisp under his breath.

'She had a swimming pool, a beauty salon and a massage room. There was a ballroom, a theatre; quoits and curling decks . . . A veritable floating palace she was,' he said, twitching his moustache and looking round the table mournfully. 'A palace fit for royalty. Why, I remember dining on roast pheasant stuffed with Orcadian truffles, followed by champagne and macadaccio nut ice cream, with King Adolphus and Queen Rita at this very table. What a night that was! Let me see, there was the renowned portraitist Rachel Dubois, the famous pot-holer and musical dramatist Edward T. Trellis, Dame Ottoline Ffarde . . .'

Just then, there was a hissing sound from above,

followed by a groaning sound from below, and the tables – Crane & Sons Automatic Self-Serving Tables – began to shake. Then, one after the other, the silver covers in the middle of each table shot up towards the ceiling to reveal three circular trays, laden with bowls, rising up from below.

Captain Belvedere reached forward and took a steaming bowl. He sniffed at it sadly. 'Tomato soup,' he said gloomily. 'Whatever would Queen Rita say?'

# 3. Deck Croquet

*H*e's here, the one with the green head and the creaking feet. The water he gives me is stale, but I am too thirsty to care.

*Oh, how I miss the little girl who used to come, and the cool, dark places in the palace gardens that only I knew.*

*Now he is giving me the sweet white petals. One . . . two . . . three . . . They are delicious, and for a moment I can forget that I'm trapped inside this hollow tree.*

'Really, dear?' said Mrs Flood distractedly. 'How interesting.'

But Corby knew that she hadn't found what she'd been saying interesting at all. In fact she was beginning to doubt whether her mother had registered a single word she'd told her about the sad song that she had heard the day before. Ever since Corby had come and sat in the deckchair next to her, Mrs Flood had been rummaging through her large battered handbag.

'So what do think it could have been?' Corby persisted.

'Been?' her mother repeated vaguely.

'Yes, the noise,' said Corby. 'The song—'

'Oh, not just now, darling,' said Mrs Flood, flicking her hair back over her ears and rummaging all the more feverishly. 'Where *is* it?' she said irritably.

'What are you looking for?' asked Corby.

'That school prospectus,' came the reply.

Corby sighed.

The school prospectus . . . That shiny blue booklet which told parents like Corby's what a wonderful, well-equipped and well-run place Harbour Heights School was. It was the reason Mr and Mrs Flood were so keen to send her and her brothers there.

Corby had never been to school before. In Dandoon, all the Flood children had been taught at home by personal tutors. Now, after their father's great disappointment, all that was going to change.

'I'm sure I put it in my bag this morning,' Corby's mother was saying. 'I distinctly remember laying it down, opening my bag and— Oh, bother!'

All at once, Mrs Flood had had enough. She cranked the mechanical deckchair forward and tipped up the bag. The contents spilled out across the deck all around her tortoiseshell sunglasses with gold wing-tips, a silver compact, several tubes of lipstick, a clutch of keys, a book of matches, an assortment of crumpled handkerchiefs . . . as well as the bizarre selection of buttons, coins, tickets, safety pins and fluff that lies at the bottom of every bag. A hundred items or more there must have been, but the school prospectus was not one of them.

'You put the school prospectus down?' said Corby.

'Yes,' her mother said. 'I put it down and opened my bag and—' Just then, the quiet of the late afternoon was shattered by the sound of loud voices and pounding feet.

'Defilade to the offside, Cedric!'

Mrs Flood and Corby looked up, just in time to see a red and blue striped wooden ball go spinning past them, with Cedric, Hubert, Ernest and Toby – all laughing uproariously – hurtling after it, their mallets raised.

Cedric reached the ball first, and hit it firmly. With a loud *clack!* it bounced off the metal stanchion in front of him and spun up into the air.

'Spike on!' he roared. 'Fire in the hold!'

'Watch the birdie!' shouted Hubert and Ernest together, as the ball reached its highest point in the air and then sped back down to the deck.

Toby barged past his older brothers, arms outstretched. 'Dunroamin'!' Corby's youngest older brother bellowed as his fingers closed around the ball. He turned to his brothers. 'Second wicket to me, I think you'll find,' he said.

'Certainly is,' said Cedric.

'Well played, sir!' said Hubert.

'Brilliant catch,' said Ernest. 'As crisp as a Gibbons shirt!'

And the three older boys clustered round their youngest brother, slapping him enthusiastically on the back.

'Congratulations, Toby!' said Corby, jumping to her feet and clapping louder than any of them.

'Oh, hello, sis,' said Toby, grinning back at her. 'I didn't see you there. Fancy joining in? You could be the outside flank-sweeper.'

'No thanks,' said Corby, who could never quite get the hang of her brothers' games. 'I was just . . .'

But her words were lost in the sudden burst of cheering and jeering as Hubert snatched the ball from Toby's grip and threw it up in the air.

'Mr Jolly's gone to market!' he bellowed, and thwacked the ball as hard as he could with his mallet.

'What a dream of a backhand!' shouted Ernest as he belted after the ball, Cedric and Toby in hot pursuit.

As the riotous game reached the end of the deck, the boys skidded round the corner and disappeared, and the sound of their excited voices faded. Mrs Flood turned to Corby, her eyes twinkling with pride and happiness.

'My little boys,' she sighed.

Corby smiled back. At fifteen, fourteen, thirteen and twelve, Cedric, Hubert, Ernest and Toby were hardly 'little boys' any more, and to Corby herself, of course, they'd always seemed big. But to Mrs Flood they would always be her 'little boys'.

Just then, the young lieutenant, Jon-Jolyon Letchworth-Crisp, appeared from the opposite direction.

'Dear, dear,' he said, standing above them, his hands on his hips as he surveyed the contents of the empty bag lying in a pile all around them. 'I know that deck sports can be a bit boisterous, but the way your sons play—'

'Oh, no, no, no,' said Mrs Flood, standing up and flapping her hands. 'That wasn't them. It was me. I was looking for—' She stopped and took a sharp intake of breath. 'The school prospectus,' she said to Corby. 'I quite forgot—'

'But, Mother—' said Corby, shaking her head.

'It went right out of my head in all the excitement,' Mrs Flood was saying. 'I had it this morning. I distinctly remember coming out, putting it down on the deckchair, opening my bag and—'

'Mother, it's right there,' said Corby. 'You've been sitting on it the whole time.'

'Don't be ridiculous, dear. Of course I haven't. I'd have—' She paused. 'I was?'

Corby nodded. 'Here it is. Harbour Heights School,' she said. 'A little creased around the corners.'

'Well, thank goodness for that,' said Mrs Flood, smiling warmly. 'Oh, Corby, darling, you're such a treasure. I really don't know what I should do without you.' She winked. 'Now, if you could just help me with all this mess here,' she said.

Corby was about to help her mother, but Jon-Jolyon beat her to it.

'Let me, Mrs Flood,' he said. 'It's the least I can do for suggesting that it might have been your sons who caused the mess in the first place. Such charming boys, all of them. A credit to you, if I might be so bold.' He began gathering up the items and returning them to the bag. 'As indeed are *all* your children.'

'Thank you,' said Mrs Flood. 'It's very kind of you to say so.'

'Harbour Heights School – an excellent institution from what I hear, Mrs Flood,' said Jon-Jolyon smoothly, eyeing the prospectus in Mrs Flood's hands. 'Though for children as charming and talented as your own, my dear Mrs Flood,' he continued, 'surely personal tutors would be the obvious choice?'

'I'm afraid, Lieutenant–' said Mrs Flood.

'Please, call me Jon-Jolyon,' said Jon-Jolyon with a smile.

'I'm afraid, Jon-Jolyon,' Mrs Flood continued, 'after my husband's . . . er . . . disappointment, I'm afraid personal tutors would be far too expensive.'

'Oh, I understand, Mrs Flood,' said Jon-Jolyon, suddenly serious. 'As for myself, I don't intend to remain a humble lieutenant for much longer. I have great plans, Mrs Flood . . .'

Corby had heard enough. 'I'm going for a walk,' she said, and set off along the deck.

As she came to the metal stairway that led to the upper deck, she heard Jon-Jolyon's voice: 'One day I'm going to be a captain, and not of an old rust-bucket like the *Euphonia*, but of a *real* ocean liner . . .'

The upper deck, Corby was pleased to see, was

empty. No noisy brothers. No whispering Hattenswillers. No odd man from Cabin 21 – nor any of those sinister men in their smart suits and bottle-green bowler hats.

Corby couldn't help shivering whenever she thought about them. They seemed, on the surface, to be very polite, raising their hats and bowing their heads to everyone they met. But it had been very different that first day on board, when Corby had accidentally bumped into the tall one in the yellow checked suit. He had tripped over one of the automatic parasols on the deck, which had sent him sprawling, followed by his four companions, like a set of deck skittles. Corby hadn't meant to, but they looked so funny that she couldn't help laughing. The tall gentleman had leaped to his feet, his face contorted with rage.

'Nobody laughs at the Brotherhood of Clowns!' he'd hissed.

Corby had been so shocked that she'd stopped laughing instantly, and it was only after they had slunk away that she noticed the small gold-edged card lying on the deck. She'd picked it up and turned it over.

MR TIMES-ROMAN, M.A.A.C.M., it read. MASTER OF THE ANCIENT ART OF COMEDIC MIME.

Corby had slipped the card into her copy of *Hoffendinck's Guide*. That had been three weeks ago.

MR TIMES-ROMAN
M.A.A.C.M.
*Master of the Ancient Art of Comedic Mime*

Leaning against the safety rail on the starboard side of the ship, Corby rested her chin on her folded arms and watched the turbulent line of froth trailing away from the back of the boat. To her right, the sun was sinking down to the horizon. To her left, far in the distance, she thought she could see a stretch of land glinting in the golden light. It looked intriguing.

She opened *Hoffendinck's Guide* . . .

and be sure to look out for the dancing turtles that come ashore during thunderstorms.

# THE COAST OF DALCRETIA

One of most remote and mountainous coastlines in the world, the Dalcretian coast boasts many stunning natural harbours and delightful little towns. Long favoured by small pleasure-boats and yachts, recently larger vessels have stopped to sample the delights of Dalcretia.

The thick pine forests and mountain peaks are home to the formidable Dalcretian shepherds, who tend their flocks in lonely isolation for years at a time, before coming to the coast for the extraordinary Dalcretian holiday festival known as 'The Longest Afternoon'.

Each Dalcretian coastal town boasts of its own 'Longest Afternoon' as the best of its kind, and often spends years preparing for one.

## SIGHTS TO LOOK OUT FOR:

*Doral's Mountain Goats* – can be spotted leaping from the highest crags. Look out also for the dwarf tree-climbing goats and the extremely shy cave-dwelling goats.

*Dalcretian shepherds* – with their distinctive black cloaks and impressive moustaches, the Dalcretian shepherds are renowned for their extraordinary strength, stamina and lack of conversation.

# NOTES

## Harbour Heights School

| Good points | Bad points |
|---|---|
| Make new friends | having to make new friends |
| interesting lessons | boring lessons |
| Mother and father will be pleased if I do well! | bossy teachers |
| | having to do as I'm told |
| | The head mistress (sounds like a dragon in the prospectus!) |
| | School uniform - YUK! |

Me in uniform!!!

Corby let the pencil go. It dangled from the string around her neck.

There was the beautiful coast of Dalcretia, with all its interesting sights – which she would never see, Corby thought miserably. All *she* had to look forward to was rotten old Harbour Heights School.

She closed *Hoffendinck's Guide* with a heavy sigh.

# 4. The Brotherhood of Clowns

*'ve been trapped in this tree for so long I'm beginning to forget . . .*

*The palace gardens, the little girl who comes when the cymbal sounds, and the dappled sunlight in the quiet corners . . .*

*Everything.*

Corby wasn't sure what made her do it. Perhaps it was the creaking footsteps coming up the metal stairway, or the sound of whispering voices, or the flash of bottle-green she'd glimpsed for a split second. Whatever it was, she had known instantly that she didn't want to be discovered here, alone, on the upper deck – especially by the Brotherhood of Clowns.

Desperately, she looked around. Where could she hide?

Under that deckchair? Too obvious. Behind the chipped white funnel? They'd spot her straight away. What about . . . ? Yes! That was it, the lifeboat. Of course!

Corby clambered over the side of the lifeboat that swung, suspended, just above her, and pulled the tarpaulin cover over her head just in time. The sound of creaking shoe leather came closer, and the whispers grew louder.

'Nope, you must be mistaken, Bembo, me old mate. Ain't nobody up 'ere and that's a fact,' said a gruff voice.

Corby shivered.

'But Franklin-Gothic,' came a soft, slightly wheezy voice, 'there was definitely someone here, standing at the railings . . .'

'Eez not 'ere now, no way,' came a third voice, high-pitched and impatient.

'That is correct, Palatino. We are indeed alone. Now gather round. You too, Garamond. Stop daydreaming and pay attention!'

Corby recognized the sinister voice of Mr Times-Roman.

MR. GARAMOND

'Sorry, boss,' came a fat, chewy voice that obviously belonged to Mr Garamond. 'It's just that I can 'ear it singing – 'ere in me 'ead – the saddest song . . . And it's beginning to get to me!'

Corby gasped. So the clowns knew all about the saddest song!

'Oh, stop your whining,' said Franklin-Gothic nastily. 'After all, we've done the 'ard part, ain't we, boss? Just got to keep it nice and quiet until . . .'

MR. FRANKLIN-GOTHIC

In the lifeboat above, Corby's heart was beating so hard she was amazed that the Brotherhood of Clowns couldn't hear it. They seemed to be clustered at the railings just beneath.

MR. BEMBO

'Quiet, the lot of you,' hissed

46

Times-Roman menacingly. 'For your information, Franklin-Gothic, the "'ard part", as you put it, certainly isn't over. And as for you, Garamond, pull yourself together. Saddest song indeed! It's all in your mind. Remember, we're the Brotherhood of Clowns. What are we?'

*'The Brotherhood of Clowns!'* chorused the other voices.

'And we fear nothing,' Times-Roman went on, 'except . . .'

'A slow handclap and a well-aimed custard pie!' replied the others in unison.

'That's right!' said Times-Roman. 'So don't you forget it! If we pull this little job off for the headmistress, we'll be rich, brothers! Rich, do you hear me?'

'We hear you, brother,' said the others.

'No more ringmasters and acrobats looking down their noses at us. No more warming up the audience for the knife-throwers and plate-jugglers. No, if we succeed, then we'll own the circus. We'll call the shots – and we'll see who's laughing then!'

The brotherhood broke into sinister sniggers.

'All we have to do is keep our eyes and ears open, and if we spot anyone snooping . . .'

'Or sniffing around,' added Garamond.

'Or sneaking about,' said Bembo.

'Or skulking in ze corners,' added Palatino.

'Or eavesdropping!' hissed Franklin-Gothic.

'Then we all know what'll happen to them, don't we, brothers?'

Corby couldn't see, but she was sure that the sound she could hear was the sound of four bottle-green bowler hats nodding. Her blood ran cold.

'That's right,' whispered Times-Roman. 'An accident. A very nasty accident.'

# 5. The Unfortunate Cabin Incident

 lone. All alone, here in this hollow tree. The forest floor still sways, and the sun doesn't shine . . .

'So I had a word with that nice young lieutenant,' Mrs Flood was saying a little distractedly as she fiddled with her hair in front of the mirror. 'And *he* had a word with the peculiar gentlemen - what did you say they called themselves, dear?'

'The Brotherhood of Clowns,' said Corby, aghast. 'But, Mother! I told you not to say anything!'

It was the worst possible thing that could have happened. She'd crept out of the lifeboat as soon as the Brotherhood of Clowns had gone, her heart thumping, and rushed back to the safety of her

parents' cabin. She hadn't
wanted to say anything,
but her mother had
taken one look at her
ashen face and trem-
bling hands and insisted
that she tell her the
whole story.

'But now they'll know
that I was eavesdropping!'
Corby protested.

'Oh, I shouldn't worry
about that, dear,' said her
mother sweetly, 'because
as those funny gentlemen
explained to Jon-Jolyon, what
you overheard was simply a
rehearsal. Some new routine they're working on. They
had quite a laugh about it apparently. So you see, no
harm done,' her mother went on, turning to face her.
She pulled her hair up and twisted it round. 'Up?'
she said. 'Or down?' She let the hair tumble down
over her shoulders.

'Down, I think,' said Corby miserably. 'Yes, definitely down.'

Mrs Flood smiled warmly. 'Thank you, darling,' she said, twisting it back up on top of her head. 'Oh, and while you're here, perhaps you'd like to try and persuade your father to get out of bed and have dinner with us this evening. It seems that nothing *I* say has any effect on him. After all, we've got to learn to make the best of things and try to stay cheerful!'

With the Brotherhood of Clowns on her trail, Corby felt anything but cheerful – but she had her father to think about.

'I'll give it a go,' she said with a weak smile, 'but I'm not sure it'll do any good. After his disappointment, Father doesn't seem to listen to *any* of us any more.'

'Well, do your best, there's a good girl,' said Mrs Flood cheerfully.

Winthrop Flood was the most brilliant engineer of his generation, renowned for building some of the most famous bridges in the world – bridges Corby had seen in the large photograph album he kept on the desk in his study.

There was the majestic eight-span steel-arch bridge which crossed the Terinaki Gorge, the MacDonald Bluff suspension bridge, the Hootenanny Falls bridge, the Lafayette cantilever bridge over the Hoobly River – and the famous bascule

TERINAKI GORGE

bridge at South Bay Gap, designed to be raised so high that even the largest ships could enter the Shadrak Channel.

His latest, biggest and most impressive project had

MACDONALD BLUFF

been the Tamberlaine-Marx Crossing, a series of inter-connecting bridges linking East Point to Western Reach across the Dandoon Delta. From the outset the work had been hampered by the mosquitoes infesting

HOOTENANNY FALLS

the swampland and hindered by the unpredictable tides.

Many said it could never be done. But Corby's father had been determined to prove them all wrong and earn the title of the greatest bridge builder in the world.

LAFAYETTE CANTILEVER

And he would have – Corby was convinced of it – if it hadn't been for a very tiny but extremely important thing called an ampersand escalating threading-bolt.

BASCULE BRIDGE

Usually, Winthrop Flood personally designed and supervised the construction of every single item used in the building of his bridges. But the week they were making the ampersand escalating threading-bolt, Corby had had a bad case of the croup (she was only a year old at the time) and Winthrop had taken some time off.

Seven years later,

TAMBERLAINE-MARX CROSSING

the magnificent Tamberlaine-Marx Crossing was ready for opening, and the Begum of Dandoon, in her best hat, was standing with a pair of solid gold scissors ready to cut the pink ribbon and declare the crossing open. The whole family was there, and Corby could remember how proud of her father she had felt.

And then it had happened. The ampersand escalating threading-bolt had failed to escalate.

This was very important, but not being a brilliant engineer like her father, Corby wasn't sure why. What she *did* know was that it was a very bad thing, because the Tamberlaine-Marx Crossing made a sound like a sinking fire engine and slowly – as if a herd of invisible elephants were having a jumping competition on them – the inter-connecting bridges trembled, lurched, writhed and arched sharply upwards. The next moment there came a series of loud *cracks* as the bridges began breaking in two, one after the other, until the entire crossing was one big wreck.

The Begum was very understanding and said that it was nobody's fault, but Winthrop Flood couldn't help blaming himself. Following that fateful afternoon he

had not looked at a blueprint, picked up a pencil, or even gone near a spanner. In fact, Corby's father had taken to his bed. He had only got up once since the great disappointment of the Tamberlaine-Marx Crossing disaster, and that was to come on board the S.S. *Euphonia* for the voyage home to Harbour Heights.

Once they arrived there, Mr Flood had announced, he would retire from bridge-building for ever. He was no longer going to travel with his family round the world, but instead would work for his brother-in-law, H. H. Luscombe, designing umbrellas – and his children were going to attend school whether they liked it or not.

Corby knocked on the bedroom door. 'Father,' she called, 'are you awake?'

'Go away!' came the gruff voice from inside. Corby decided not to ask him about the snuff just now.

'Like a bear with a sore head,' said Mrs Flood. She turned to her daughter. 'You'd better go and get ready yourself. Off you go now, darling,' she said as cheerfully as she could manage, but Corby could see that there were tears in her eyes.

Corby went to her own cabin, which she shared with Serena, and pushed open the door. It was small compared to her parents' suite, but it still took her breath away. It was one of the S.S. *Euphonia*'s self-tidying cabins which, when the ship was new, had been an even greater marvel than the mechanical deckchairs on the starboard deck.

In the self-tidying cabins, everything

folded neatly away – beds, tables, cupboards, wardrobes, shelves, bookcases, shoe-racks, wall-lights and ceiling fans, even the framed pictures on the wall – until the cabin was an empty box. The fun part was pressing the buttons and switches on the wall to make everything appear. Even though Corby had already been on board the S.S. *Euphonia* for three weeks, she still hadn't got tired of it.

She reached out and pressed the button nearest her, and a fully made bed lowered itself silently from the wall. Corby sat down on it with a contented sigh and reached out to press the button for the bedside table.

*Boing!*

The metallic sound echoed loudly through the cabin, as the bed abruptly flipped upwards, and Corby was tossed into the air.

*'Aaarrgh!'* she cried out as she found herself being propelled across the room.

*'Youch!'* she hollered as she slammed into the wall opposite and a tiny bathroom swung out.

As it did so, a shower head appeared from above and sprayed water down upon her, ice-cold and full-blast.

'*Aaiiii!*' Corby screamed, spinning round and tripping over a foot-spa.

From the wall behind her, an array of items suddenly sprang out. There was a mechanical toothbrush, buzzing and scrubbing at thin air, a hair-dryer blowing hot and cold, and a magnifying shaving mirror which captured the bewildered expression on her face as it went in and out, in and out, on an extending arm.

'Stop it! Stopffmmth—' Her cries were smothered by the volley of cotton-wool balls being launched from a protruding nozzle.

All at once there was a loud hiss, and an eau-de-Cologne dispenser flew towards her, spraying the air with sweet perfume. Corby staggered backwards, tripped over the automatic trouser press which had slid out from the alcove next to the doorway, and landed with a thud on the bed.

As she did so, there was a second loud *boing!* followed by a *clunk* and a *hiss*, and the bed flew upwards again, this time slamming shut against the wall – and trapping Corby inside. Outside in the cabin, Corby could hear a hissing sound, like a kettle

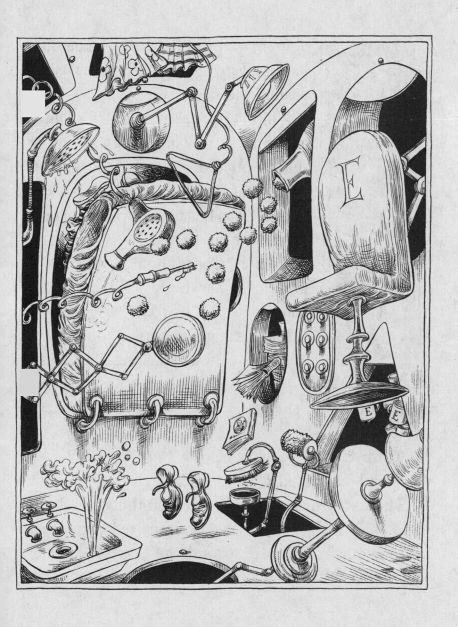

coming to the boil, getting louder and louder. With all her might, she pushed against the bed.

It didn't open, but it shifted slightly, allowing her just enough room to thump on the padded wall she was pressed against. On the other side of the wall was her parents' cabin, where her father lay in bed.

'Father!' Corby shouted with all the breath in her body. 'Father! Help! *Help!*'

The hissing was getting louder, and the walls of the cabin were beginning to rattle and shake. From the other side of the wall she could just make out her father's voice.

'Corby?' it was saying. 'Corby? Is that you?'

'Help!' screamed Corby. 'HELP!'

There was the sound of bumps and things crashing, and then a big jolt as the door to the cabin was thrown open. The next second she heard her father bellowing, 'Stand back!' and the confined place she was trapped in filled with a scraping, scratching and scrabbling, and the sound of screws being hurriedly undone.

Suddenly, there was another loud *hiss*, followed by a *click,* and the bed lowered itself elegantly to the floor.

'Corby!' an excited and relieved cry went up, and everyone gathered round her. There was her mum (her hair up) and her dad (in crumpled pyjamas), Cedric, Hubert, Ernest and Toby – and, at the back, Serena. The next moment everyone was asking questions at the same time.

'I don't know . . . I haven't a clue . . . I don't have the foggiest idea . . .' she answered one after the other. 'One minute everything was fine, the next it all went wild. The shower, the mirror, the cupboards, the bed . . .'

Mr Flood, who had been examining the pipes and gauges and electrical circuitry in a small concealed box to the right of the door, tutted loudly.

'Looks like the steam pressure,' he said, and shook his head. 'It was lucky the whole lot didn't blow up.'

As his words sank in, everyone in the room fell

still. The thought of what *might* have happened was too horrible!

'Problem is,' said Mr Flood, looking down, as if surprised to see the spanner in his hand, 'the whole ship's been so badly neglected over the years, it was an accident just waiting to happen . . .'

Everyone looked at each other, then back at Mr Flood.

'Anyway,' he said, clearing his throat, 'since I'm out of bed now, perhaps I'd better make myself useful and check out a few more things while I'm about it. After all, I'm *still* an engineer – not an umbrella designer. At least, not just yet.'

Everyone gathered round him, laughing and smiling. Only Corby noticed the sinister figure walking past the open door, and glancing in briefly before continuing along the corridor.

It was Mr Times-Roman, leader of the Brotherhood of Clowns.

# 6. Love Fish

'm so tired. Now I shall close my eyes and sleep. Perhaps, when I wake up, I'll be back in the palace gardens and the palace cymbal will sound, and the little girl will come . . .

Captain Belvedere poked his head round the cabin door and waggled his moustache mournfully.

'Dreadful business,' he said to anyone who would listen. 'Something similar happened to Binky Beiderbecker, as I recall, just after the Halfway-There Ceremony on our maiden cruise. Never went near another cocktail shaker again . . .'

Behind him, the concerned face of Lieutenant Jon-Jolyon Letchworth-Crisp appeared. 'What a shambles!' he exclaimed. 'My dear Miss Flood, are you harmed in any way?'

Jon-Jolyon pushed past the captain and clasped Serena by the hand.

'I'm fine, silly,' she smiled. 'It was Corby who—'

'Thank goodness!' exclaimed Jon-Jolyon. 'Now, come away from that mess this instant. I'll get Arthur to see to it.'

He turned and led Serena away, his voice echoing down the corridor: 'Arthur! Arthur! Where are you, blast your eyes! *Arthur!*'

Just then, the gong sounded for dinner.

'Come along, everyone,' said Mrs Flood brightly. 'We mustn't let a little accident spoil our appetites.'

Corby shivered. She was far from convinced that it had been 'a little accident', as her mother put it. The Brotherhood of Clowns was behind this, she was sure of it. But who was going to listen to a little girl? What Corby needed was proof.

'Oh, and Winthrop, dear,' her mother was saying as she noticed her husband's crumpled pyjamas. 'Do go and change into something a little more suitable.'

'What's that, dear?' said Mr Flood, looking up from a tangled mass of pipes and wires he was pulling from the wall and examining. 'Yes, yes. Won't be a moment

. . . Just checking . . . Ah, yes . . . *Mmmm . . .*'

Mrs Flood gave an exasperated shrug. 'Cedric! Hubert! Ernest! Toby! Time for dinner!'

'I could eat a horse,' said Cedric, following his mother.

'I could eat a camel,' said Hubert.

'I could eat an elephant!' exclaimed Ernest.

'And I,' cried Toby, 'could eat a whole whale!'

They trooped out of the cabin.

'How about you, sis?' called back Hubert.

'Oh, I'm not very hungry,' said Corby. The last thing she felt like was having dinner with the Brotherhood of Clowns. 'I think I'll go on deck for a little bit.'

She left her father happily dismantling the cabin and went up onto the top deck.

It was a perfect night. The air was balmy and still, and the sea was like a millpond. Corby lay back on a padded deckchair and stared up at the hazy spread of twinkling stars above her head. Then she picked up her pencil and opened *Hoffendinck's Guide . . .*

# TOWNS OF THE DALCRETIAN COAST

### FEDRUN

The pretty coastal town of Fedrun is renowned for its pancakes and sweet cucumbers. Wander through its winding cobbled streets and soak up the quaint, rustic charm.

A FEDRUN

The hat-making district is particularly interesting. Don't miss the chance to have your head measured and fitted for a 'fedrun' – the famous conical hat worn by the local fishermen.

THE DANCING PIG

See also the famous dancing pig of Fedrun, which is reputed to know over two hundred different dances, and performs at Fedrun's riotous 'Longest Afternoon' festivities.

208

# NOTES

STARS

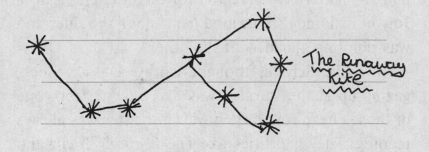

The Runaway Kite

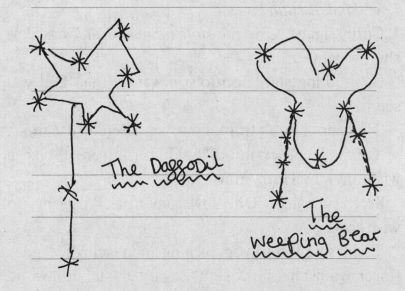

The Daffodil

The Weeping Bear

'Oh, look!' came a voice from her left.

Corby closed *Hoffendinck's Guide* and looked across the deck, and there – leaning against the safety rails and bathed in the flickering light of the ship's hanging lanterns – were Jon-Jolyon and Serena. Jon-Jolyon had one arm around her sister's shoulder and was pointing ahead with the other.

How like Serena, thought Corby. Out on deck, gazing up at the stars. It was like a scene from one of those cheap romantic novels her sister was always reading. They had titles like *The Yearning Heart* and *Love Finds Letitia*.

Corby sighed. Give me *Hoffendinck's Guide* any day, she thought.

'A shooting star,' Jon-Jolyon was saying. 'Did you see it?'

'N . . . no, I don't think I did,' said Serena dreamily.

'Oh, well, never mind,' said Jon-Jolyon. 'Make a wish anyway. Hurry now . . .'

Serena giggled. 'Oh, how romantic. I'm going to wish for—'

'Sssh!' said Jon-Jolyon, turning and placing his index finger against her lips. 'Don't say it out loud or it won't come true. Besides, Serena, at the risk of flattering myself, I think I *know* what your wish is . . .'

'How conceited,' Corby muttered to herself.

Jon-Jolyon leaned forwards, his eyes closed, until his face was inches from Serena's.

Just then, there was a faint hissing sound as a dazzling white meteor appeared out of nowhere and sliced down through the sky.

'Look! Another shooting star!' cried Serena, clapping her hands with excitement. 'Did you see it?'

Jon-Jolyon opened his eyes. 'Y . . . yes,' he said.

But Corby knew he hadn't.

'Now it's *your* turn to make a wish,' said Serena.

'I wish . . .' said Jon-Jolyon, leaning closer to Serena once more, 'that . . .'

'Oh, Letchworth-Crisp!' came Captain Belvedere's voice, floating up from the dining room. 'Letchworth-Crisp! Come quickly! There seems to be a problem with the automatic tables. There's rice pudding all over the ceiling . . . Letchworth-*Crisp!*'

'It's that Arthur's fault!' muttered Jon-Jolyon tetchily. 'Still, what can one expect from a third engineer? I'll be back as soon as I can,' he told Serena as he strode off.

Serena turned back to the sea. Far away, down on the horizon, the full moon was beginning to appear. A golden sliver it was at first, which grew as it rose, until a shimmering light stretched out across the ocean towards them like a yellow-brick road. Corby was just about to join her, when she heard a strange clanging noise just behind her.

She spun round, heart racing, half expecting to see Mr Times-Roman and the Brotherhood of Clowns. But instead, she caught sight of a sooty head poking out of a rusty funnel.

'Sorry if I startled you, miss,' said the head, which was smiling and, Corby could see as he clambered out of the funnel, belonged to a young man in grubby overalls. 'The name's Arthur.'

The young man held out a grubby hand.

'So *you're* Arthur!' said Corby. 'The third engineer!'

'That's right, miss. Pleased to meet you – although not so much third engineer as *only* engineer on this old tub. As well as ship's cook, ship's doctor and ship's dogsbody. Just can't get the crew these days!'

He gave her a dazzling smile, and Corby couldn't help smiling back.

'I was just checking this intake duct because – I don't know if you've noticed, miss, but we've been having a little trouble in the galley.'

'Please call me Corby,' she said, shaking his hand. 'And you're *not* the only engineer on this tub. My father's an engineer, too – and a very good one at that!'

'Really?' said Arthur. 'Is that a fact? Well, you tell him from me, Miss Corby, that if he ever feels a little rusty and fancies keeping his eye in, then there's a poor, harassed, overworked third engineer who could certainly do with some help!'

Arthur turned and made for the stairway down to the lower deck.

'I will, Arthur,' she called. 'As soon as he's finished mending my cabin.'

But Arthur didn't hear her. He'd stopped stock-still in mid-stride and was staring at Serena, who was standing a few feet away, beside the safety railing where Jon-Jolyon had left her. The silvery moonlight was glinting on the waves and, as Arthur and Serena's eyes met, the sound of a thousand tiny, flapping wings filled the air.

They turned and
looked out to sea just
as a great shoal of
de Witt's Moonlight
Flying Fish leaped
out of the waves in a
shimmering silvery
arc, then disappeared again. For a
moment neither of them spoke.
Then Arthur held out his hand.

'Arthur,' he said in a croaky
voice.

'S . . . S . . . Serena,' whispered Corby's sister,
shaking his hand.

'Amazing!' said Corby, rushing across to them.
'Did you see them?'

'What?' said Serena and Arthur dreamily, without
taking their eyes off each other.

'There,' said Corby, pointing out to sea. 'Love fish!'

# 7. The Mysterious Clunk

*he sound, it echoes through the forest.
It woke me, here in this hollow tree. I was
having such sweet dreams of the palace
garden . . . But now I can't sleep.
The sound is getting louder . . . And I am afraid.*

*CLUNK!*

Corby woke up and yawned. She was in a hammock because, despite her father's assurances, she still didn't entirely trust that bed of hers. Besides, the hammock – which Cedric had found in the deck sports locker – was wonderfully comfortable.

*CLUNK!*

There was that sound again. Corby was just about to jump out of the hammock and go and investigate when there was a knock, and Mrs Flood popped her head round the cabin door.

'You've missed break-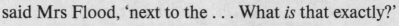
fast, so I've brought you
some elevenses,' she said,
producing a plate of
chopped-up pineapple and
watermelon, and a glass of
chilled coconut milk.

'Thanks,' said Corby.

'I'll put it down here,'
said Mrs Flood, 'next to the . . . What *is* that exactly?'

'A foot-spa,' Corby mumbled, sitting up.

*CLUNK!*

'Do you know what that noise is?' she asked her
mother, taking a sip of the coconut milk.

'That?' said her mother cheerfully. 'That is what
your father calls "a mysterious clunk". It started in
the galley last night. Oh, Corby!' she went on. 'You
certainly missed quite a dinner!'

Mrs Flood burst into a peal of laughter and clapped
her hands together.

'One of those automatic tables in the dining room
went mad, just as we were about to have dessert!

Those peculiar gentlemen in their smart suits were absolutely covered in rice pudding. Furious, they were! I shouldn't have laughed really, but I couldn't help it. Nor could the boys. And Captain Belvedere couldn't stop apologizing. That nice young lieutenant said it was all Arthur's fault, and that that was what you got if you had to rely on a third engineer.'

'Arthur?' said Serena, appearing in the doorway. 'Oh, I'm sure it can't be Arthur's fault.' She crossed to the porthole and looked out dreamily. 'It must be awfully difficult keeping a funny old ship like this going.'

*CLUNK!*

'That's just what your father said, Serena. He's down in the engine room with Arthur right now, trying to sort out this "mysterious clunk".' She smiled. 'And I must say, he seems like a changed man. I've never seen him so cheerful.'

'That'll be Arthur's influence,' said Serena, tracing a capital A on the glass of the porthole with a finger.

'Yes, well,' said Mrs Flood, giving her elder daughter a quizzical look. 'I'll be on the starboard deck if you need me, girls. Your brothers are playing marine rugby on the lower deck, so I'm keeping well clear. Oh, and your young lieutenant has agreed to join them – though goodness knows why.'

Serena turned to her mother, her eyes flashing. 'He's not *my* young lieutenant, Mother!'

*CLUNK!*

Mrs Flood left and Serena turned back to the port-hole. In the distance, a rocky coastline was just visible. Corby jumped out of her hammock and joined her sister.

'It looks so romantic,' said Serena. 'I wonder what it's called?'

'That's the Dalcretian coast,' said Corby. 'According to *Hoffendinck's Guide* it's full of all sorts

of interesting places to visit and fascinating things to see.'

'Yes, but *we* can't visit any of them,' said Serena, 'because this stupid, rusty old ship doesn't stop anywhere any more!'

*CLUNK!*

'And poor, sweet Arthur has to spend all his time in the horrid old engine room trying to keep it going!' Serena added crossly. 'I hate the S.S. *Euphonia*!'

*CLUNK!*

Serena turned and stamped out of the cabin. Corby reached for a pencil and opened *Hoffendinck's Guide* . . .

# TOWNS OF THE DALCRETIAN COAST

### MESAPOLI

Mesapoli nestles inland on the banks of the River Mesa. The twenty bridges over the river are all worth a visit, as are the small houses on either side.

The inhabitants of Mesapoli are notable for being extremely small, with few of them more than four feet tall. This they more than make up for by being extremely tough, and they are feared by other Dalcretians because of their short tempers. Luckily, they are also wonderfully hospitable to strangers – so long as no one mentions their height.

MESAPOLITANS

Mesapoli's other claim to fame is their renowned wheezing donkey. The creature is reputed to be able to cough 'The Lament of St George', the Dalcretian national song.

THE WHEEZING DONKEY

214

# NOTES

## Arthur

| Good points | Bad points |
|---|---|
| Good Looking | a bit messy |
| hair not too greasy (I think) | only just met him so can't be sure if he's always cheerful |
| Smiles a lot | works too hard |
| works very hard | is only a third engineer. |
| is very cheerful | |
| is an engineer! ✓ | |

A town with twenty bridges, thought Corby. How her father would love that . . .

*CLUNK!*

This time the whole ship seemed to shudder, and then lurch sharply to starboard and back again. Corby shut *Hoffendinck's Guide*, hurriedly dressed, and rushed out to discover what exactly was going on.

# 8. Mechanical Deckchairs

*ark, so dark. I can remember nothing . . .*

'Clear the decks!' shouted Hubert, launching the marine-rugby ball high into the air across the lower deck.

'Hugger-mugger!' Ernest, Cedric and Toby replied, linking arms and forming a tight circle.

Corby stepped back out of the way as the ball landed in their grasp and turned to see Jon-Jolyon stick out a sneaky foot and send Hubert sprawling.

'Hugger-mugger!' shouted Ernest, Cedric and Toby together as they threw the ball back towards their brother, only to see Jon-Jolyon seize it triumphantly, stick it up his jumper and sprint past Corby to the marine-rugby net.

'Nice try, boys,' he smirked. 'But just not good enough!' He bounced the ball into the empty net. 'My round, I think!'

The Flood brothers looked at each other. Hubert rubbed his shin and stood up, and shook Jon-Jolyon's hand.

'Thought I had that game in the bag,' he said ruefully, though from his expression it was clear he knew Jon-Jolyon had cheated. 'Sure as a Lemuel sneeze on washday.'

'Can't win 'em all,' said Jon-Jolyon suavely and, spotting Corby, strode over to join her. 'Ah, Miss Flood,' he said, smiling. 'Where might I find that beautiful sister of yours? I'm sure she'll be impressed to learn I not only survived, but triumphed in a game of marine rugby with these brothers of yours.'

Corby managed a faint smile. 'She'll be on the starboard deck with my mother, I expect.' She frowned. 'I was just wondering about that clunk—'

'Starboard deck, you say?' said Jon-Jolyon, pushing

86

past. 'As for the "clunk", that's Arthur's headache, not mine. I certainly don't intend to get my hands dirty!'

Corby flushed pink. She hadn't been sure about Lieutenant Jon-Jolyon Letchworth-Crisp at first, but now she positively disliked him. 'Well,' she said, following the lieutenant up the stairway towards the starboard deck, 'Serena didn't seem to mind Arthur's dirty hands when they met last night . . .'

Letchworth-Crisp stopped and turned; his eyes narrowed. 'Met last night?' he repeated.

'Yes,' said Corby. It was her turn to push past the lieutenant. She made her way onto the starboard deck. 'They met last night after you left,' she called over her shoulder. 'Like two love fish, they were!'

She marched over and sat down on the mechanical deckchair next to her mother, who appeared to be asleep under a large floppy straw hat. In one hand she clutched her large handbag, in the other, an opened copy of the Harbour Heights School prospectus.

That'll show Lieutenant Jon-Jolyon Letchworth-Crisp, thought Corby. Perhaps he won't be quite so smug now.

She reached down and pressed the lever on the side of the deckchair. It had the words CRANE & SONS SELF-PROPELLING NAUTICAL CHAIR on the side in embossed letters. There was a faint wheezing sound as the deckchair rose on its mechanical legs and walked stiffly across the starboard deck. Corby let go of the lever and, with a soft creak, the deckchair came to a halt.

A little way off, the Hattenswillers – in their conical hats and long coats – sat in deckchairs of their own, deep in conversation. Every so often Mr Hattenswiller would scribble on tiny pieces of paper and pass them to his wife, who would examine them with an air of great secrecy, before turning them over and scribbling on the back in turn. Back and forth the pieces of paper went, as they whispered to each other in their funny voices, all the while casting furtive glances in the direction of the foredeck.

What on earth were they up to? wondered Corby.

'Whiffl-whif-whif-whiffl,' said Mrs Hattenswiller.

'Mummer-mmm-mmum-mum,' replied Mr Hattenswiller.

When they saw Corby, they hurriedly hid their notes and raised their hands in greeting.

'Whiffl-whif-whif?' said Mrs Hattenswiller.

'Mum-mummer-mmum?' said Mr Hattenswiller.

'No, thank you,' said Corby. 'I've just had elevenses ...'

'Whif?' said Mrs Hattenswiller, puzzled.

'Mummm!' said Mr Hattenswiller, shrugging his shoulders.

Corby pulled on the lever. The deckchair lurched forward and set off, past the puzzled Hattenswillers, round the corner onto the foredeck and—

She let go of the lever, and the deckchair rattled to a halt.

Mr Times-Roman looked up, a thin smile playing

on his lips, his own Crane & Sons Self-Propelling Nautical Chair blocking her path.

'Well, well, well,' he said, in his dry, sinister voice. 'If it isn't our little eavesdropper.'

'The snooper . . .' hissed Mr Franklin-Gothic, his mechanical deckchair appearing on one side of Corby's own.

'The sniffer . . .' added Mr Garamond, guiding *his* deckchair to the other side.

'The sneaker,' said Mr Bembo.

'Ze skulker,' added Mr Palatino, as the pair of them brought their deckchairs up behind her.

Corby swallowed hard. The Brotherhood of Clowns had her surrounded. Five pairs of cold, hard eyes stared at her, unblinking; five thin, cruel smiles sent shivers along her spine. Reaching down gingerly, Corby's hand closed round the lever of her deckchair. She gave Mr Times-Roman her biggest, brightest smile.

'Oh, very good! Very good!' Corby laughed through gritted teeth. 'This must be the new routine you've been working on!'

She pulled the lever on her deckchair, which let out a rusty squeal and leaped forwards, shunting Mr Times-Roman and Mr Garamond aside. Corby clattered across the fore- deck as, behind her, five mechanical deckchairs screeched round on protesting legs and gave chase.

'Follow that deckchair!' Mr Times-Roman's sinister voice rang out. 'Cut her off at the prow!'

Corby was horrified to see Mr Bembo and Mr Palatino gallop past her and swerve round to block her path. She yanked the lever hard to the left, sending her chair spinning round, and came face to face with Mr Times-Roman; Garamond and Franklin-Gothic by his side.

'Trapped, like a second-rate acrobat on a wonky trapeze,' laughed Mr Times-Roman triumphantly.

Corby shut her eyes tight and thrust the lever forwards as far as it would go. With a tremendous *crash!* she smashed into Times-Roman's chair.

*'Oomph!'* gasped Mr Times-Roman, as his chair promptly folded up – with him in it.

Corby leaped to her feet and dashed across the foredeck. From behind her came the sound of splintering wood and angry shouts as, one after the other, the clowns crashed into the wreckage of her own mechanical deckchair. Corby didn't look back.

Now you lot know what it feels like, she thought as she sprinted round the corner and onto the port deck. She didn't stop running until she arrived back at her mother's deckchair, gasping for breath.

'Taking some exercise, darling?' said her mother brightly, without looking up from the school prospectus she was reading. 'That's nice.'

Corby flopped down into the deckchair beside her and tried to catch her breath. A few moments later there was the sound of loud groaning, followed by raised voices and creaking wood, as the Brotherhood of Clowns appeared from the direction of the foredeck.

They were carrying the mechanical deckchair, jammed shut, with Mr Times-Roman sandwiched inside. As they passed Mrs Flood, they shot dark looks at Corby, but tipped their bottle-green bowler hats at her mother all the same.

'Oh, my!' said Mrs Flood, looking up from beneath the brim of her floppy straw hat, and trying to stifle a giggle. 'You gentlemen are certainly unfortunate! First the dining-room table, and now this . . . Oh, do forgive me,' she said, bursting into laughter. 'But you do look so funny . . .'

'Nobody . . . *umph!* laughs at . . . *umph!* the Brotherhood of Clowns . . .' grunted Mr Times-Roman, going red in the face as the Brotherhood of Clowns man-handled the folded deckchair down the stairway to the lower deck.

'Easy, boss,' said Mr Franklin-Gothic. 'Try not to speak. We'll find that third engineer, and he'll soon get you out of this.'

As the clowns disappeared, Mrs Flood returned to the Harbour Heights School prospectus.

'Well I never! Fancy that!' she exclaimed a moment

Headmistress L
Blackletter, B.F
M.M., O.L.S.C.,
pictured here
world-famous
of handmade
exotic hand
welcomes
Harbour H

later. *'Headmistress Lucida Blackletter, B.F., A.C., M.M., O.L.S.C., D.D.D., pictured here with her world-famous collection of handmade shoes and exotic handbags,'* she read, *'welcomes pupils to Harbour Heights School.'*

She held up the prospectus for Corby to see.

Corby sighed. She hadn't much liked the idea of going to that school in the first place, but the look of the hollow-eyed, thin-lipped headmistress, with her shoes and handbags made from dead animals, gave her the creeps.

She shuddered as she opened *Hoffendinck's Guide* and picked up her pencil . . .

# TOWNS OF THE DALCRETIAN COAST

### LISSARI

Built on the side of steep granite cliffs, Lissari is one of the most charming and picturesque of the towns of Dalcretia. With its excellent 'hanging taverns' and 'suspended kitchens', eating and drinking in Lissari is a unique experience for anyone with a head for heights.

A LISSARI TURBAN

The cave shops of the Eastern District sell beautiful hand-woven fabrics which are worn by local women in the famous Lissari turbans, some measuring more than five feet across.

THE COUNTING OX

Dancing is the local pastime in Lissari, but visitors must be careful if attending cliff-top dances.

Lissari is also well known for possessing a remarkable counting ox, which lives in a large cave at the foot of the cliffs.

# NOTES

'Mind if I sit down?' came an oily voice.

Corby closed *Hoffendinck's Guide* and looked up. Serena was sitting three deckchairs along, reading a well-thumbed copy of *The Handsome Horseman*. Jon-Jolyon Letchworth-Crisp was standing over her.

'If you must,' said Serena quietly.

Letchworth-Crisp smiled smoothly. 'Thank you,' he said, settling himself in the deckchair next to her. 'Because I think we ought to have a little chat . . .'

# 9. The Marshmallow Trail

*One white petal, sweet and delicious. I eat it, and then wait for the next. But it doesn't come. The one with the green head and creaking feet goes away.*

*I am alone once more . . .*

*Perhaps if I sing I can let the sadness out, and my heart will not break . . . Just yet.*

Corby got up, walked casually over to the safety railing and pretended to be very interested in the coast of Dalcretia. Not that she *wasn't* interested in the coast of Dalcretia. It was just that, right now, she was more interested in hearing what Jon-Jolyon had to say to Serena, but didn't want to appear to be listening too obviously.

A little way along the deck, she noticed the man

from Cabin 21. He was sitting, as usual, in his deckchair, staring, as usual, out to sea and wearing, as usual, his navy-blue deck shoes, his white suit and dark glasses. He too was looking as if he wasn't listening to Jon-Jolyon and Serena's conversation.

'I hear you met Arthur last night,' said Jon-Jolyon casually.

'The third engineer?' said Serena, turning pink. 'Yes – he seemed very nice.'

'Oh, yes,' said Jon-Jolyon with a bitter little laugh. 'He does seem nice, doesn't he?'

'What do you mean?' said Serena, sitting up, her face flushed and her eyes flashing.

'My dear girl.' Jon-Jolyon sounded as suave and smooth as ever. 'It's just that I would hate to see you making a fool of yourself.'

'And why should I do that?'

'Well, a little bird told me that you and Arthur were like a pair of love fish last night . . .'

Corby suddenly noticed an extremely interesting mountain peak in the far distance and examined it minutely, while she felt her cheeks flushing even redder than her sister's.

'And what if we were?' stormed Serena. 'What's that got to do with you?'

'Serena, please,' said Jon-Jolyon, laying a spotlessly clean hand on her arm. 'I'm only trying to help. You don't know Arthur like I do. There's only ever been one true love in his life, and he'll never leave her . . .'

Serena pulled her arm away, but she was clearly hanging on Jon-Jolyon's every word. 'Who?' she breathed.

Jon-Jolyon laughed. 'Why, the S.S. *Euphonia*, of course!'

Serena smiled, getting up to leave. 'Oh, I think I can handle the *Euphonia*.'

'That's what all the girls say,' said Jon-Jolyon airily, examining his fingernails.

'*All* the girls?' said Serena, sitting down again.

'Oh, did I forget to mention the girls?' said Jon-Jolyon smoothly. 'Yes, Arthur has one in every port. Of course, if you ask him, he'll deny it. But one thing he can't deny is that he'll never leave the *Euphonia* – whereas I, on the other hand, have great plans. Why, I was telling your mother only the other day . . .'

But Serena was no longer listening. She had

104

jumped to her feet and dashed to the safety railing, her jaw set and her eyes wet with tears . . .

And then an extraordinary thing happened. The man from Cabin 21 got up out of his deckchair, rummaged in the pocket of his white suit and pulled out a handkerchief (which was also white, with an

embroidered blue H in the corner) and handed it to Serena. Then he walked slowly away.

Jon-Jolyon leaped up, waving his own handkerchief (which was red with white polka dots), but Serena rushed past him and fled back to her cabin, holding the white handkerchief to her eyes. Corby turned on her heel, gave Jon-Jolyon a furious look, and strode off along the deck.

She was just going down the stairs when her left foot landed on something soft, squishy and extremely sticky.

'*Yuk!*' she exclaimed, lifting her foot and examining it.

Long, gloopy strands of glistening white stuff were strung out between the deck and the bottom of her deck shoe. She looked more closely, poking tentatively at the goo and putting her fingers to her nose. They smelled of sweetness and vanilla.

'A marshmallow,' she muttered, her top lip curling. 'How disgusting.'

It wasn't that Corby didn't like marshmallows. Sometimes, when they all went camping, she and her brothers would stay up half the night, telling each other ghostly stories and toasting marshmallows. They had tasted delicious. A marshmallow on the bottom of your shoe, however, was something else – particularly on a day so hot that it had turned it to a sticky mess.

Corby opened *Hoffendinck's Guide* and very carefully tore off the corner of the 'Notes' page. The picture of a laughing goat on the page opposite caught her eye. She paused a moment as she read the words above it . . .

107

# TOWNS OF THE DALCRETIAN COAST

### DORALAKIA

The small, isolated town of Doralakia is widely regarded as the hidden jewel of the Dalcretian coast. Situated on the very tip of the Dalcretian peninsula, the lights from its extraordinary tower houses are a familiar sight to passing ships.

The tower houses of Doralakia are to be found nowhere else, and are well worth a visit, as is the pretty little harbour with its friendly tavern and small grocery store.

The Doralakians are among the most hospitable and friendly of all the Dalcretians. Their 'Longest Afternoon' festival is the most elaborately celebrated in all Dalcretia, and is especially famed for the appearance of the town's remarkable laughing goat.

THE LAUGHING GOAT

224

# NOTES

What an interesting place, thought Corby, closing the guide.

Using the scrap of paper, she scraped the marshmallow off the sole of her shoe as best she could, and continued – the tackiness catching on the floor with every step. At the stairs, she looked down and frowned. A second marshmallow was lying there. A pink one.

Picking it up, Corby continued down the stairs, only to find a third marshmallow – another pink one – lying on the half-landing between the two flights. She paused thoughtfully.

One dropped marshmallow could have been an accident, two dropped marshmallows looked like carelessness – but three, well, that was a trail, and Corby found herself searching around for others. Sure enough, halfway down the next flight of stairs were two more – one white and one pink – stuck together and nestling in the corner. She picked them up, too.

On the next deck down Corby saw a white marshmallow lying in the middle of the scuffed decking, and a second one a little further along, and a third a little further after that. She looked down, and took a sharp intake of breath.

The trail of marshmallows seemed to be leading to a door just down from Cabin 21. Corby followed the trail, gathering the marshmallows as she did so, until she came to the door. Then, with her heart beating louder than ever, she seized the door handle and turned it. The door swung open and Corby stepped inside, to find herself . . .

. . . in a broom cupboard!

For a moment she stood there, surrounded by mops and brooms and buckets, with a handful of marshmallows in one hand and *Hoffendinck's Guide* in the other, feeling pretty stupid.

And then she heard it. The saddest song, rising and falling, like a sad wolf singing to the moon, or a lonely songbird calling to its mate – and it seemed to be coming from somewhere very close by.

Corby reached out and pushed the wall at the back of the broom cupboard. Except it wasn't a wall. It was another door – heavy, made of metal, and ever so slightly ajar. Holding her breath, Corby leaned forwards and peeked into the room beyond.

At first she could barely make anything out. But slowly, her eyes became accustomed to the gloom.

She saw a huge, shadowy storeroom, stacked high with hessian sacks, tea chests and labelled boxes, and enormous varnished sea chests, some of which she recognized as belonging to her own family. As for the saddest song, it seemed to be coming from a row of large wooden crates in the far corner of the cargo hold.

As quietly as she could, Corby stepped through the broom cupboard door and into the dark hold. She tiptoed through the maze of cargo, scarcely daring to breathe, until she came to the wooden crates. Something rustled at her feet and the singing abruptly stopped.

Looking down, Corby noticed a large paper packet with a hole in the bottom. She nudged it with her shoe. It was empty. Then she heard the sound of breathing and snuffling and, looking up, she saw something between the slats of one of the large wooden crates.

It was a big, sad, doleful eye, and it was looking straight at her.

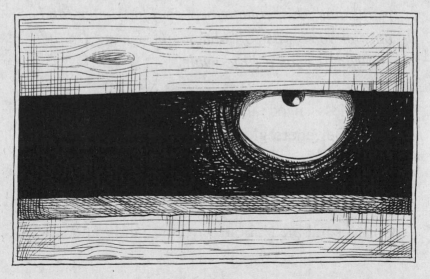

# 10. The Halfway-There Ceremony

*he heard my song and she came. A little girl came. Not the little girl from the palace gardens, but another little girl. There were tears in her eyes.*

*She gave me white petals, lots of sweet white petals, and whispered to me. I couldn't understand, but her voice was soft and soothing. And I didn't feel sad . . . for a little while.*

'A little less speed and a little more caution,' said Captain Belvedere gloomily, climbing to his feet.

'I'm sorry, Captain,' said Corby, who had been sneaking out of the broom cupboard and run straight into him.

Corby scrabbled about on her hands and knees,

picking up *Hoffendinck's Guide* and several bits of paper that had fallen out of it. There was Mr Times-Roman's card, a leaflet showing the correct way to use the foot-spa in her cabin, her ticket stub, a crumpled photograph of the Tamberlaine-Marx Crossing taken just before it collapsed and . . .

'I believe you dropped this, little girl,' said Captain Belvedere gloomily, handing her a half-torn label that had stuck to his shoe.

'Yes, thank you,' said Corby, taking it – secretly grateful that the captain hadn't thought to read it.

She opened her *Hoffendinck's Guide* and hastily stuck the label on a blank page . . .

# THE HALFWAY-THERE CEREMONY

The origins of the 'Halfway-There' Ceremony are as mysterious as the ceremony itself. Instituted aboard the S.S. *Euphonia* on her maiden voyage, it has been faithfully carried out on each subsequent ocean crossing, a tradition that has spread to other ships. Legend has it that failure to observe the ceremony will result in the vessel never reaching its destination, and being condemned to sail the ocean for ever, perpetually 'halfway there'.

The ceremony itself involves the crew and passengers donning fancy dress and having a big party. Traditional games such as 'Blind Mermaid's Buff' and 'Musical Icebergs' are played late into the night to appease the sea god Neptune and his wife 'Flotsam Florrie', who are played by the captain and the first officer.

SOME SUGGESTED FANCY DRESS COSTUMES:
The Dancing Pig of Fedrun
A Captain's Uniform
A First Officer's Uniform
A Mermaid
(Anything really except a clown costume, as this is considered very bad luck.)

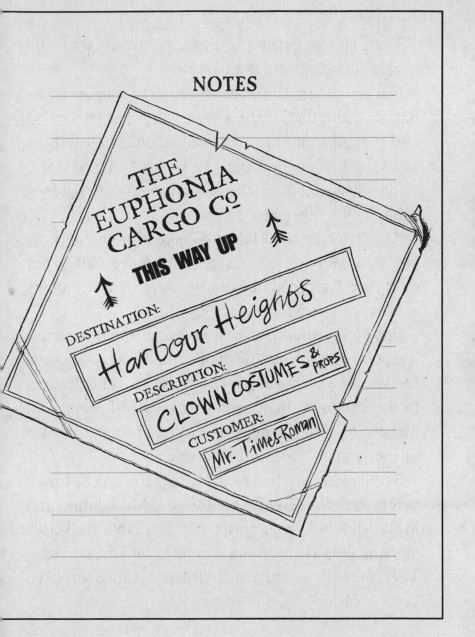

Then she snapped *Hoffendinck's Guide* shut and smiled innocently at the captain.

Corby had torn the label off the large wooden crate. She was sure that, if she showed it to her father and told him all about the creature locked inside and the sad song it sang, he would know just what to do.

She dashed off in the direction of her parents' cabin at the other end of the ship.

'Don't forget the Halfway-There Ceremony, little girl,' Captain Belvedere's gloomy voice called out after her. 'Everybody has to be there. No exceptions – even for me. More's the pity . . .'

But Corby didn't hear him because she was too intent on looking out for the Brotherhood of Clowns. Luckily, she managed to reach the corridor leading to the cabins without seeing any sign of them, and was just breathing a huge sigh of relief when the door to the laundry room clanged open.

She skidded to a halt as Mr Times-Roman, followed by Mr Franklin-Gothic, Mr Bembo, Mr Palatino and Mr Garamond (who was holding a large packet of marshmallows in his hand), stepped into the corridor. They were all wearing their freshly laundered suits, which seemed to have shrunk several sizes in the wash.

Mr Times-Roman turned stiffly to face Corby. Round his neck he wore a large brace. He took a step towards her, his green bowler hat wobbling on his head, his fingers twitching and his tiny jacket bunching up round his shoulders.

'So,' he snarled, 'we meet again—'

Just then, there came a loud peal of laughter. With a grunt of pain, Mr Times-Roman spun round.

'Oh, I'm so sorry!' squealed Mrs Flood. 'It's just that you gentlemen have no idea how funny you look!'

She tried in vain to stifle her laughter as she bustled past the scowling Brotherhood of Clowns and took Corby's hand.

'There you are, darling! I've been looking for you everywhere!' she giggled. 'If you don't hurry up, you'll be late for the Halfway-There Ceremony – and we can't have that, can we, gentlemen?'

The brotherhood raised their green bowler hats, but Mr Times-Roman's smile was as thin as paper as Mrs Flood ushered Corby into her cabin and closed the door. From inside the cabin there came the sound of helpless laughter.

Mr Times-Roman grimaced. 'Nobody laughs at the Brotherhood of Clowns,' he snarled, 'and gets away with it!'

The gramophone on the foredeck was wound up and the sound of Dame Ottoline Ffarde singing 'Daisy's Lament' filled the warm night air for the umpteenth time. Beside it, an extraordinary-looking individual in a long green wig and skirt, and carrying a trident, reached out a hand and raised the needle. The strange array of dancers in front of him froze as the music stopped.

A plump man dressed up in a large cardboard seashell wobbled unsteadily on one foot.

'You moved!' said Lieutenant Jon-Jolyon Letchworth-Crisp, pointing his trident.

Mr Garamond, who was meant to be a spitting whelk, looked up and started to shuffle off.

'No, not you!' said Letchworth-Crisp. *'You!'*

Arthur, who was standing as still as a rock and looking extremely handsome in a crisp white first officer's uniform, shrugged.

'If you say so, Flotsam Florrie!' he laughed. He went to sit on a deckchair beside a table on which a large plate lay, piled high with sardine sandwiches. Next to it stood an equally large jug of coconut milk with

NEPTUNE'S TIPPLE written in red letters on the side, and a huge tureen of cold rice pudding with a flag on the top, which read FLORRIE'S BLANCMANGE.

'It's "Sir" to you,' said Jon-Jolyon, with all the dignity he could muster and, adjusting his tangled green wig, he placed the gramophone needle back on the record.

'*Oh, sweet Alfred, my heart is breaking . . .*' sang the voice of Dame Ottoline Ffarde on the crackly record.

. . . And my feet are aching! thought Corby as she attempted to dance – which wasn't easy, especially as she was dressed as a bumblebee (her mother's idea) and being stared at by five disgruntled clowns, who were dressed up as Lemuel Gibbons and four spitting whelks.

122

The music stopped again.

'You, you, you and you!' said Jon-Jolyon, pointing to Mr Garamond, Corby, Mrs Hattenswiller (who seemed to be dressed as a teapot) and the man from Cabin 21 who had come as, Corby guessed, the Dancing Pig of Fedrun, although she couldn't be certain.

That just left Serena, who was dressed in a dazzling white gown with silver thunderbolts in her hair, and a sash across her shoulder emblazoned with the words SPIRIT OF THE *EUPHONIA*.

'You win,' Neptune told her gloomily from his deckchair throne, which was festooned with gold cardboard seashells. 'I suppose Neptune and Flotsam Florrie have been appeased, but we'd better have one more game of Blind Mermaid's Buff,' he said, 'just to be on the safe side . . .'

Corby groaned. This was the worst party she'd ever

been to. For a start, nobody was allowed to touch the food. 'It's purely symbolic,' Jon-Jolyon had pointed out snootily, which was just as well, because it was also horrid. What was more, there were only two party games, both of which were excruciatingly dull, and which they'd had to play over and over again, 'to appease Neptune!' as Jon-Jolyon had reminded them all.

Beside her, the Flood boys were just as bored. They'd dressed up as their sporting heroes. Cedric was 'Buffy' Mandrake, the deck-croquet ace. Hubert was L. P. Smythe of the Old Mustardians. Ernest was 'Flim-Flam' Andrews, the table-lacrosse champion. And Toby was Teddy Luscombe, who'd taken a record twenty-three wickets only last season.

Serena seemed to be avoiding Arthur, and her father – dressed in Dalcretian national dress, with an oversized fedrun – was too distracted to talk to, since he was listening out for the 'mysterious clunk' and doing calculations on the back of his hand. Only Mrs Flood seemed to be having a good time. She was swaying about in a giant Lissari turban and flowing skirt, teasing the Brotherhood of Clowns,

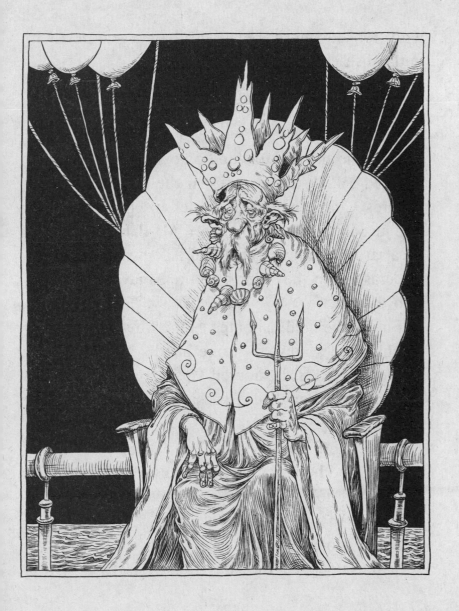

who looked more peculiar than ever in their outlandish costumes.

'Blind Mermaid's Buff,' announced Jon-Jolyon, placing a paper bag over Mr Palatino's head and spinning him around.

Everyone else had to stand on one leg. Mr Palatino sneaked a look out of a rip in the bag and tiptoed towards Corby, muttering under his breath. Corby was just about to scream, when Mr Palatino slipped on a sardine sandwich that had fallen from the table. He crashed to the floor and the sandwich shot up into the air.

'Fire in the hold!' shouted Hubert, leaping up and catching the sandwich in one hand.

'Well played, sir!' shouted Cedric.

'Shall we?' laughed Ernest, and the others all nodded.

'Food fight!' Toby yelled.

The Flood boys grabbed handfuls of sardine sandwiches and dollops of cold rice pudding, and Arthur picked up the jug of coconut milk.

'I say!' protested Jon-Jolyon. 'That food is—'

Arthur upended the jug over Flotsam Florrie's

head. 'Purely symbolic!' he laughed.

A hail of sardines and soggy bread flew through the air as the Hattenswiller teapot and teacup ran for cover, and bumped into the Dancing Pig of Fedrun. Mrs Flood shrieked with laughter as the Brotherhood of Clowns fled a rain of cold rice pudding.

'Nobody laughs at the . . . *ppubl!* . . . *plubb!* . . . *pplub!*' spluttered Mr Times-Roman as a dollop hit him squarely in the face.

Mr Flood didn't seem to notice the sardine stuck to the side of his fedrun hat as he furiously worked out the sprocket ratio of the Wibbler mesh-wheel. Serena strode off to her cabin, followed by a dripping Jon-Jolyon.

'Boys will be boys!' laughed Mrs Flood. 'They're just letting off a bit of steam. After all, it *is* meant to be a party.'

'Whiffl-whiffl,' said Mrs Hattenswiller.

'Mmum-mumm,' said Mr Hattenswiller.

The Dancing Pig of Fedrun adjusted his dark glasses and walked off in the direction of Cabin 21.

'Neptune is satisfied,' declared Captain Belvedere gloomily, pulling off his cardboard crown. 'I declare the Halfway-There Ceremony over!' He wiped his brow. 'And thank goodness is all I can say . . .'

The Flood boys and Arthur gave a cheer.

'Time for bed,' said Mrs Flood cheerfully. 'You too, my little bumblebee,' she said to Corby. 'It's been a long day.'

'But I wanted to show Father—' Corby began, opening *Hoffendinck's Guide*.

'By jingo! I've got it!' cried her father, examining the equation on the back of his hand and rushing over to Arthur. 'Arthur, me lad!' he said. 'Get changed. We've got a long night ahead of us!'

Corby looked on as the pair of them strode away. Her mother took her by the hand. 'Whatever it is, dear,' she said, 'I'm sure it'll keep till morning.'

'I hope so,' said Corby, looking around the now deserted foredeck. 'I certainly hope so.'

# 11. Cabin 21

*S*he came when I sang. The little girl came and gave me the sweet white petals, and whispered to me . . .

But then she went away, and the sadness has returned. Perhaps if I sing again . . .

When Corby got back to her cabin, Serena was still dressed as the Spirit of the *Euphonia*, though her silver lightning bolts were lying on the floor and her hair was loose and tumbling over her shoulders. Corby could see she'd been crying.

'What is it, sis?' asked Corby, sitting down gingerly on Serena's bed. She still didn't quite trust the beds in the cabin, despite Mr Flood's repairs.

'Spirit of the *Euphonia*,' said Serena with a bitter laugh, tearing off the sash and letting it drop to the floor beside the lightning bolts. 'That's a good joke.'

Corby took her hand.

'Arthur loves me, you know,' Serena continued, squeezing her sister's hand. 'But he loves this rusty old excuse for a ship more, just like Jon-Jolyon said—'

'Jon-Jolyon?' said Corby hotly. 'What does *he* know?'

'More than you think, Corby,' said Serena, tears filling her eyes. 'He's going to be a captain one day, of a proper ship – not like Arthur . . .'

Corby gave her sister a big hug. 'Perhaps, one day, Arthur might—' she began.

'No!' said Serena fiercely,

pulling away. 'He'll never leave the *Euphonia*. He told me tonight. No matter how rusty and run down she gets, and no matter how many jobs he has to do because the rest of the crew have all gone, he said he'll *never* leave. Not even . . .' She broke into uncontrollable sobs and buried her face in the white handkerchief the man from Cabin 21 had given her. 'Not even for me!'

'You never know, sis,' said Corby. 'Perhaps he'll change his mind—'

Serena turned, her eyes blazing. 'Well, it's too late now!' she said. 'Because I've finished with him.' She sniffed. 'Now, Jon-Jolyon, he's got *real* prospects. And what's more, he loves me. He told me so. I can't wait to see the look on Arthur's face when I tell him! Stupid love fish!' Serena stormed. 'What do *they* know?'

'But sis,' protested Corby. 'Not Jon-Jolyon! He's so smarmy, and he cheats at deck rugby, and—'

'I don't care,' Serena said, jumping into bed and pulling the covers over her head. 'Arthur's only got himself to blame!'

And then she began to cry again – and this time,

she didn't stop. In the end Corby picked up her *Hoffendinck's Guide* and quietly slipped out of the cabin.

That was the trouble with Serena, Corby thought. Too romantic for her own good. She believed everything she read in those silly books of hers.

Up on deck, Corby headed straight for the prow. In the distance the ragged outline of the Dalcretian peninsula was black against the dark sky and at its tip, like the candles on a great black birthday cake, lights flickered in the darkness. There were hundreds of them, glowing faintly, their light reflecting off the glittering sea. It was magical. Corby could have stood and watched them all night - and she probably would have done if it hadn't been for one thing.

The saddest song.

There it was again, very soft and far-away-sounding, but unmistakable. The creature in the crate was calling to her, Corby was certain, and she had to go to it.

She set off along the deck towards the stairs to the cargo hold, trying to make as little noise as possible - although that was difficult, she realized, when

you're dressed up as a bumblebee and your paper wings rustle. From down in the depths of the ship came clinking and clunking sounds as Arthur and Mr Flood worked in the engine room.

Tomorrow she would tell her father, Corby told herself. He would know what to do. But now she must go to the creature and comfort the poor thing. How it must be suffering, locked up in that horrid wooden crate! Corby could feel her blood begin to boil.

How could people be so cruel? she wondered. Just wait till she told her father. Then those Brotherhood of Clowns had better watch out!

She marched down the stairway towards the broom cupboard and stopped . . .

The door to Cabin 21 was open.

Corby couldn't resist it. She tiptoed up, trying hard to keep her wings from rustling, and peeked inside.

The cabin was magnificent. A huge chandelier hung from the ornately decorated ceiling, on which painted love fish swooped and darted above painted waves. The walls were lined with bookcases and beautiful inlaid panelling. Neptune and Flotsam Florrie, carved in gleaming cherrywood, seemed to be keeping guard on either side of magnificent double doors.

There were tables and glass-fronted cabinets, bristling with extraordinary objects: towering Fedrun fishermen's hats, long-necked vases and vast pots covered in intricate designs of laughing goats and counting oxen, rolls of sumptuous fabric and round, cork-stoppered jars of sweet cucumbers and honey.

At the centre of all this, in a high, wing-backed

chair, slumped forwards and snoring softly, sat a man in a pig costume. On the small table next to him was a half-empty bottle whose label read, FINEST DORALAKIAN COOKING SHERRY, and a picture in a silver frame of a beautiful, dark-eyed woman.

Corby was just about to tiptoe away, when she noticed something even odder. The bookcases were full of leather-bound books that she recognized straight away.

'*Hoffendinck's Guides*,' she whispered. 'Hundreds of them.'

# 12. Midnight in the Cargo Hold

*hat is that? Is it the little girl? Has she come in answer to my song?*

*I can't see. It is too dark in the forest and I can't move in this hollow tree . . .*

'What was that?' whispered Mr Garamond.

'What was *what*?' hissed Mr Franklin-Gothic nastily.

'That noise,' said Mr Garamond. 'Sounded like a sneeze. It came from over there somewhere . . .' He lifted his lamp towards a pile of crates in the far corner of the cargo hold.

'I didn't hear anything,' said Mr Franklin-Gothic with a sneer. He shook his head. 'You're letting this 'ere job get to you, Gary, old son.'

137

'Can't help it, Frank,' said Mr Garamond, giving the wooden crate they were standing in front of a sharp kick. 'It's the noise it makes. It really gets to me. I can't get it out of my 'ead . . . It makes me so sad . . .'

'You'll be a lot sadder if old Romey hears you talking like that. Now give it those marshmallows and let's get out of here,' said Mr Franklin-Gothic.

Mr Garamond bent over and picked up the paper bag beside the crate. 'That's funny,' he said. 'The last bag had a hole in it, and now *this* bag is half empty.' He looked round furtively. 'Must be rats. I knew I shouldn't have left it here—'

'Never mind,' snapped Franklin-Gothic. 'Just get on with it. This place gives me the creeps.'

'One . . . two . . .' counted Mr Garamond, pushing each marshmallow through the space between the wooden slats, 'three . . . four . . .'

138

'Steady on, Gary,' said Mr Franklin-Gothic. 'The boss said no more than three at any one time, remember.'

He reached down and took the fourth marshmallow from Mr Garamond's hand and held it up to the lamplight between his thumb and forefinger. He gave it a little squeeze and whistled through his teeth.

'There's enough sleeping powder in one of these little babies to put you to sleep for a week, Gary, me old mate, so take it easy.'

Mr Garamond got to his feet and kicked the crate again. 'At least it's not singing any more,' he said.

Just then, there came the sound of jangling keys from the direction of the door.

'Time to make ourselves scarce, Frank,' whispered Mr Garamond.

'You read my mind, Gary,' replied Mr Franklin-Gothic, turning off his lamp. 'Just don't go tripping over any mops on the way out. And stop those shoes of yours creaking!'

As the two clowns disappeared into the broom cupboard, the door to the cargo hold, marked CABINS 22–40, swung open and Captain Belvedere shuffled in. Behind him trooped two enormous men in baggy trousers and grubby vests. Each had a large black moustache and wore a long red cap with a tassel on the end of it.

'Hurry up, you two,' Captain Belvedere was saying gloomily. 'We haven't got long. After all, I shouldn't even be stopping here.'

Not that you could call slowing down to offload a few crates 'stopping' exactly. But the owners of the S.S. *Euphonia* certainly wouldn't have liked it, whatever it was called. Still, what they didn't know wouldn't hurt them, Captain Belvedere reasoned, and besides, Mama Mesapoliki paid him well for 'not stopping exactly' so that her two sons could bring their boat out to the ship and pick up her goods.

'The passengers' cargo is clearly marked,' Captain

Belvedere said to the men slowly and clearly, as if talking to two young children. He pointed to a diamond-shaped label on the side of one of the tea chests. 'So leave all those ones with labels where they are. Do you understand?'

The two men nodded their heads, and the tassels on their red caps danced up and down.

'Your crates are over there,' Captain Belvedere continued, 'in the part of the hold which used to be Cabin thirty-seven's sunken bath and spa fountain . . .' His eyes took on a faraway look and he twitched his walrus moustache from side to side. 'A marvel of marine plumbing, it was. Queen Rita herself bathed her spaniel, Mitzi, in it. Insisted on coconut milk, as I recall . . .'

The two men exchanged puzzled looks.

'Without labels, we take,' said the first one.

'With labels, we leave,' said the second.

'Excuse me?' said Captain Belvedere in a distant voice, gazing into the shadows.

'Is all right,' said the two men. 'We understand.'

Corby opened one eye. MULLIGAN'S PATENT BAKED BEANS AND CHIPOLATA SAUSAGES, she read. She opened her other eye. In front of her, nestling in the straw, was an ancient and slightly rusty tin, its label faded but still legible. Corby turned over.

Something was digging into the small of her back. She reached round, pulled another rusty tin free and inspected the label.

'NUMERICAL SPAGHETTI,' she read.

Where was she? She sat up and bashed her head on the lid of the crate. Of course! It all came flooding back to her.

After she had tiptoed past Cabin 21, she had tiptoed right into the broom cupboard – placing a mop across the door in case anyone followed her – out of the other door and into the hold. The creature had stopped singing as soon as she'd whispered to it, and she'd fed it some of the marshmallows that she had found in a paper bag beside the crate.

Then, licking the powdery sugar off her fingers, she'd picked up her pencil and was just about to write in *Hoffendinck's Guide*, when there was the loud clatter of someone tripping over the mop in the broom cupboard.

Quick as a flash, Corby had rushed over and

climbed into the first crate she could find with a loose lid. The fact that it appeared to be filled with nothing but straw hadn't puzzled her at the time. She'd been far too concerned about being discovered by those nasty clowns. The straw had tickled her nose, and she'd had to stifle a sneeze – but luckily, they hadn't heard her.

They'd spent ages whispering to each other, but Corby couldn't make out a single word. Besides, she was feeling so sleepy all of a sudden that she could hardly manage to keep her eyes open. In fact she hadn't managed it, because she must have fallen asleep right there in the straw-filled crate.

Only it wasn't just filled with straw. It was also filled with rusty tin cans. Corby rummaged about and pulled out a couple more.

OLD MOTHER LEONARD'S PRUNES AND CUSTARD, she read, and HINKEL'S BEST MEATBALLS IN GRAVY.

Well, thought Corby, can't lie here all day, reading rusty tin cans.

No, she had to go and find her father straight away. She slid the lid to one side and poked her head up out of the crate – and that was when she realized . . .

She was no longer in the cargo hold of the S.S. *Euphonia.*

But if she wasn't, thought Corby, then where on earth was she?

# 13. The Hundred-Years-Old Grocery Store

*S*uch a beautiful dream . . .

*I am back in the palace garden with the warm breeze on my skin. Soon, the little girl will come with sweet meadow grass and honey flowers . . .*

*I don't ever want to wake up.*

Corby climbed out of the crate. She found herself at the top of a tall pile of them, in what seemed to be some sort of shop – although Corby had never seen a shop quite like it.

She clambered down the crates, and sneezed. The place was so dusty. A fine layer coated everything: the floor, the shelves that surrounded her and the shuttered windows through which a thin shaft of light pierced the sparkling, dust-filled air.

Over in the far corner was a large, ornately carved counter, with the oldest cash register Corby had ever seen at one end, and an enormous pair of brass scales at the other. In between was a tall pyramid of tin cans that looked as if it was about to tip over and crash to the floor at any moment.

And as for the tin cans themselves . . .

Corby looked about her. Never in her life had she seen so many tin cans in one place. The shelves were stacked, floor to ceiling, with them. Large cans, small cans; broad flat cans, tall thin cans; cans with metal keys stuck to their lids and cans with metal screw-

tops. Some were square, others round; some corrugated, some smooth; but whatever shape or size they were, they had one thing in common. They were all rusty.

148

From the look of them, they hadn't been touched for a hundred years.

Corby looked at the faded labels. They were just like the ones in the crate she'd climbed out of.

AMBROSE'S MUSHY PEAS. WEBSTER'S BEETROOT HEARTS. GRANNY MARGIE'S HOMEMADE APRICOT BROTH. DANDOON FRUITS OF THE FOREST IN VINEGAR. DUCK OIL . . .

Just then, the door behind the counter opened and a tiny, wrinkled old lady shuffled in. She was wearing a black dress, an enormous turban and a pair of yellow-checked carpet slippers. When she saw Corby, she gave a thin, high-pitched scream and ran out again.

MAMA MESAPOLIKI

Corby could hear her shouting in a reedy voice, 'Nico! Spiro!'

And she was just about to follow her, when two enormous men with black moustaches and red caps with tassels on the end of them came striding through the door. Corby froze.

NICO

When they saw her, they stopped and stared for what seemed to Corby to be a very long time, but was in fact probably only a few seconds. Then they both threw back their heads and roared with laughter.

SPIRO

Corby smiled weakly and waited for them to finish. At last, as they dried their eyes with the back of their hands, she spoke up.

'My name is Corby Flood,' she said politely. 'Please could you tell me where I am?'

'Sorry, miss,' said one of the enormous men. 'We didn't mean to be rude, but Mama, she got a fright. She thought you were a soulopol.'

'A soulopol?' said Corby. 'What's that?'

'Is like a . . . How you say, Spiro?' He looked at his brother.

'A fairy,' said Spiro. 'A little, bad, ugly fairy. You must excuse Mama. She from Mesapoli. Very superstitious in Mesapoli.'

'Well, I'm not a soulopol,' said Corby. 'I'm a little girl in a bumblebee costume, and I'd very much like to know where I am.'

'Why, miss, you are in Mama's store. The grocery store,' said Nico.

'Yes, I can see that,' said Corby. 'But where is that?'

'In Doralakia, miss,' said Spiro.

'Doralakia?' repeated Corby, remembering what she'd read in *Hoffendinck's Guide*. 'The hidden jewel of the Dalcretian coast? With the tower houses and the pretty little harbour?'

Spiro roared with laughter and clapped his hands. 'The same!'

'With its friendly tavern? And small grocery store?'

'Yes!' laughed Nico. 'The Hundred-Years-Old Grocery Store!'

'And the remarkable laughing goat?'

The two brothers suddenly stopped laughing and looked down at their feet.

'Like we say, miss,' said Nico sadly. 'This is Doralakia.'

Just then, the little old lady came back with a large broom, and was about to chase after Corby when her two sons stopped her and explained in a long and complicated way – in a language Corby couldn't understand – that Corby wasn't a bad fairy, but was in fact a little girl in a costume. The little old lady at last seemed satisfied and, laughing, beckoned Corby to follow her.

Corby did as she was told. She followed her through the door and up a long, winding staircase that seemed to go on for ever. As she climbed, the little old lady called out in her thin, reedy voice, in the language Corby couldn't understand.

'Mama say,' called Nico, who was following them up the stairs, 'how come you in her grocery store?'

'I climbed into a crate in the cargo hold of the S.S.

*Euphonia* by mistake,' said Corby, thinking that trying to explain about the strange creature in the wooden crate would get rather complicated just now. 'And when I woke up, I was here.'

The old lady called back something else.

'Mama say,' called up Spiro, 'why you have wings and a stripy-stripy body?'

Corby sighed. If explaining exactly why she had climbed into a crate would be difficult, then explaining the Halfway-There Ceremony would be almost impossible.

'It's a bumblebee costume,' said Corby. 'It was my mother's idea.'

'Bumblebee!' laughed the little old lady uproariously. 'Bumblebee! Bumblebee!'

Finally they reached the top of the stairs, and the little old lady opened a pair of doors that led out onto a wide flat roof. Corby gasped. They were standing at the top of a magnificent tower house, surrounded by a hundred more. And in the distance, far out to sea and disappearing over the horizon, was the S.S. *Euphonia*.

Corby rushed to the far wall, waving her arms and

shouting wildly, 'Come back! Come back! Mother! Father!'

The little old lady tutted and fussed over Corby, who was battling not to break into floods of tears.

'Mama say, they cannot hear you,' said Spiro. 'But the ship, she returns with new groceries next year.'

'Next year!' wailed Corby, breaking into floods of tears.

The old lady enveloped her in strong, wiry arms and patted her head gently. 'Bumblebee, bumblebee, bumblebee,' she crooned, over and over, softly in her ear.

When Corby had calmed down a little, Mama Mesapoliki turned to her sons and spoke for a long time, waving her arms about like a tiny windmill. Spiro turned to Corby.

'Mama say you must see the mayor,' he said simply. 'He will know what to do.'

# 14. The Sad Tale of the Laughing Goat

uch a beautiful dream . . .

'If engineering has taught me anything,' said Winthrop Flood, wiping his oil-stained hands on the rag Arthur had just handed him, 'it is that the smallest things can often be the most important. Take the sprocket ratio of the Wibbler mesh-wheel, for example.'

He paced up and down the gangway of the engine room between the smoothly operating pistons.

'It was the way Hubert caught that sardine sandwich the other night that put me onto it. The way he grabbed it by the tail and sort of flicked it. Of course! I thought. It's the sprocket ratio! You see,

Arthur, the smallest things! And they can so easily be overlooked.'

Arthur smiled and followed Mr Flood along the gangway. 'Well, you've certainly got rid of that mysterious clunk,' he said. 'You've worked miracles, Mr Flood. The deckchairs are all working perfectly – not to mention the parasols and the self-adjusting railings, and as for the galley . . .'

'Oh, just tinkering, dear boy,' smiled Mr Flood. 'Just tinkering.'

'But you've taught me so much,' said Arthur in admiration. 'You've transformed the *Euphonia*. I've never seen her pistons working so smoothly. We'll reach Harbour Heights in no time at this rate, and—'

As the words left his mouth, his face fell and his mood suddenly seemed to change.

'Oh, don't mention it,' said Mr Flood happily. He turned and saw the look on Arthur's face. 'My dear chap! Whatever is the matter?' He patted the young man on the shoulder. 'You can visit us in Harbour Heights any time. You know you'll always be welcome. Serena would love it.' He smiled. 'My wife tells me she's taken quite a shine to you—'

'Oh, but it's hopeless, Mr Flood,' said Arthur, turning away and gripping the safety rail. 'I can't leave the *Euphonia*. I promised my father, after all. He's never recovered from my mother's death, and I'm all he's got . . .'

'Most commendable,' said Mr Flood, clearing his throat and fiddling with the oily rag. 'Children are such a blessing in difficult times.'

'Father! Father! Come quick! Mother wants you!' cried the Flood boys, dashing down the stairway into the engine room.

'What's all this commotion?' said Mr Flood. 'Careful of the flange-levers, Ernest! Watch those wangle-manifolds, Hubert!'

'It's Corby!' the boys shouted as one. 'She's disappeared!'


'What do you mean, "disappeared"?' said Mr Times-Roman in a quiet voice. 'How can a great big crate just disappear?'

'Dunno, boss,' said Mr Franklin-Gothic.

'Eez a mystery,' murmured Mr Palatino.

'Search me,' wheezed Mr Bembo.

'Someone had definitely been down there,' muttered Mr Garamond. 'First there was that blasted mop in the broom cupboard, then the marshmallows 'ad been tampered with . . .'

All eyes turned to Mr Garamond. Just then, from the starboard deck, came Mrs Flood's anxious voice.

'Corby! Corby! Where *are* you?'

Corby peered over the large counter and tried to stifle a sneeze.

'Mama say, if you are to take tea with the mayor,' said Nico, 'you must bring him something extra special!'

The old lady climbed a set of steps on wheels and teetered about at the top. She then reached out towards the pyramid of tin cans, swaying slightly as she did so. Corby could hardly bear to look. Surely the whole lot would come crashing down at any moment.

The old lady's hand closed around a can at the very centre of the pyramid. Slowly and gently, she pulled it free. The pyramid shuddered and creaked. The hundreds of ancient tins seemed to shift slightly and realign themselves. The whole thing tottered, but it didn't fall. The old lady held up the tin triumphantly.

'People come from as far away as Lissari just to see Mama pick a tin!' said Nico with a huge smile.

The old lady shuffled down the steps and handed Corby the dusty tin can. SNEAD AND MOPWELL'S MACARONI CHEESE IN CHEESY SAUCE, it said. Then she shuffled across to the ancient cash register and stabbed a key with a bony finger. A cloud

161

of dust flew into the air, and a NO SALE sign popped up, accompanied by a rusty *ker-ching!*

Corby sneezed.

'Come,' said Nico and Spiro together. 'We take you to see the mayor.'

Outside, the cobbled street that led down to the pretty harbour was full of black, brown and grey goats bleating loudly as several shepherds looked miserably on from their table outside a rundown tavern. Nico reached down, picked Corby up with one massive hand and placed her on his shoulders. Then they set off up the hill, through the bleating flock.

'Which one is the laughing goat?' asked Corby, looking down at the jostling, shaggy bodies.

Spiro looked up at her sorrowfully. 'None of them,' he said sadly. 'The laughing goat, she dead.' He shook his head.

'I'm terribly sorry,' said Corby, trying to keep her balance as Nico strode up the steep cobbled street.

'The Tale of the Laughing Goat,' said Nico, 'is a sad tale.'

'It bring shame and sorrow on all Doralakia,' nodded Spiro.

'What happened?' asked Corby.

'In Fedrun, they have a dancing pig,' said Nico. 'In Lissari, an ox that can count. Even Mesapoli, where Mama was born, has a donkey that can cough "The Lament of St George".'

'Here in Doralakia,' Spiro continued, 'we had the laughing goat. And people of Dalcretia, they come from far and wide to our Longest Afternoon, just to hear her laugh.'

'And what a laugh!' said Nico. 'Never was such a laugh heard, before or since.' He smiled sadly. 'And then one day . . .'

'A washday,' said Spiro.

'A washday,' nodded Nico. 'With all the clothes hanging from the washing lines between the towers.' He pointed up, and Corby saw that there were indeed washing lines stretching from one tower house to the next, far above them.

'The goat,' he continued, 'she see the mayor's trousers.'

'Trousers?' said Corby.

'Trousers,' nodded Spiro. 'High up on washing line. And she climb up to the top of his tower.'

164

'Why?' asked Corby.

'To eat his trousers, of course,' said Nico. 'What a goat!' He shook his head in admiration. 'Anyway,' he said, 'she climb his tower and reach out to take a bite . . . further and further . . .'

'And further,' added Spiro, 'until . . .'

'She fall!' said Nico, coming to a sudden halt, and almost causing Corby to topple off his shoulders. 'Right there!'

He pointed to a spot, just in front of them, outside the door of the tallest tower house Corby had yet seen.

'The mayor's house?' asked Corby.

Spiro and Nico nodded sadly.

'That's terrible,' she said. 'Dead?'

Nico nodded.

'It gets worse,' said Spiro.

'There was someone knocking on the mayor's door

when the goat, she fell,' said Nico. 'Someone very important. A great friend of the mayor, and of Doralakia.'

'Who?' said Corby.

Nico stooped and Spiro helped her down off his shoulders.

'The world-famous author of that guide you are carrying,' said Nico, pointing to the battered leather book under Corby's arm.

'Not . . .' said Corby.

Spiro and Nico both nodded. 'Hoffendinck.'

'Dead?' breathed Corby.

Spiro and Nico shook their heads. 'No, by the grace of St George,' said Spiro. 'The laughing goat, she missed him.'

'His wife, on the other hand,' said Nico. 'She not so lucky.'

# 15. Tea at the Tower House

*open my eyes and see that I am still trapped in this hollow tree. The palace gardens, the little girl – it was all a dream. A wonderful dream . . .*

*I am awake now, and still trapped . . .*

*But wait. It is not the same. The forest seems different . . . What is it?*

*My nose is tickling . . . I think . . . I think I'm going to . . . sneeze . . .*

Nico carefully approached the doorway of the mayor's tower house and took a crab-like sideways step so that he now stood with his back to the wall beside the door. He looked across at Corby and his brother.

'No one stands in front of the door,' whispered

Spiro to Corby. 'Not since Mrs Hoffendinck, she stand there, that terrible day.'

Corby nodded, staring at the mayor's front step and imagining the awful scene. Nico stretched out an arm and stiffly pulled on a heavy iron bell-pull three times. Far above her head, Corby heard the faint tinkling of a bell.

'The Mesapoliki brothers! Nico and Spiro!' came a voice. 'You have brought me a young visitor, I see.'

Corby looked round and noticed a short, ornately decorated copper and silver tube protruding from the wall. The voice was coming from it.

'The mayor,' whispered Spiro. 'He never miss a thing. If a cat sneeze in Doralakia, the mayor, he knows about it.'

'Let the young visitor in, and give my best wishes

to Mama Mesapoliki, won't you, Nico and Spiro?' said the mayor's voice.

Nico pushed the heavy wooden door open. 'The mayor, he will help you, Corby Flood,' he said, motioning her to step sideways inside. 'He a very wise man!'

Corby did as she was told. The next moment the heavy door closed behind her with a loud *creak* that echoed up inside the tower, and as it did so, the entrance hall she had stepped into was plunged into gloom.

'Climb the stairs, young visitor,' the mayor called down. 'We shall take tea on the roof. It is the custom here in Doralakia.'

So Corby began the long climb up the tower – and it *was* a long climb. A very, very long climb . . .

While the outside of the tower had been constructed from the pinkish stone that was found locally, the inside – stairs, doors and platform floors – had been made from hardwood, which had darkened to near blackness over the centuries.

The stairs wound their way up the square tower in a sort of angled spiral, with each twelve-stair flight bolted into the wall and changing direction at every corner. After six flights, Corby was already getting short of breath. By twelve, she was beginning to feel very nervous about the long drop beneath her. The only thing that was keeping her going was the sight of her destination – a ceiling that was coming closer and closer. At the top of the eighteenth flight she found herself going through a hole in the platform, and abruptly the ceiling became the floor.

'Oh no,' she groaned. 'I thought I was there!'

But she was nowhere near. On and on the flights of stairs went. Every so often, Corby would look out of one of the narrow windows, each time noting how the cobblestones of the street below had become yet smaller.

Six platforms there were in all. One hundred and eight flights. One thousand, two hundred and ninety-six stairs . . .

170

Until finally, red-faced, gasping for breath and clutching her *Hoffendinck's Guide* in one hand and the tin from the Hundred-Years-Old Grocery Store in the other, Corby stumbled into a large room. It was furnished entirely with richly patterned carpets and huge, plumped-up cushions. On the largest of these sat an old man wearing a red cap with a tassel on the end, and with the longest, whitest beard Corby had ever seen.

'Greetings, young visitor,' the old man said, his eyes twinkling. 'It is a long climb, but it is worth it, I assure you. I am Konstantin Pavel, Mayor of Doralakia. Welcome to my tower house!'

'Thank you,' gasped Corby, struggling to catch her breath after the long climb. 'My name's . . . Corby . . . Flood . . .'

'Please, follow me, Corby Flood,' beamed the mayor, standing up and deftly tucking his trailing beard over one arm to avoid treading on it. He walked across the room and flung open some double doors to reveal a rooftop even bigger than Mama Mesapoliki's.

At one corner stood an enormous telescope mounted on a sort of turntable. At the other was a round table covered with a white tablecloth with place-settings for two. The mayor motioned for Corby to sit down on one of the large cushions beside the round table. As she did so, Corby looked  out over the low wall that ran the length of the roof terrace, and gasped at the wonderful view.

Below her lay the small town of Doralakia, its

magnificent tower houses golden in the glow from the setting sun. There were hills to the north, followed by agricultural plains, with fields and orchards, and distant snow-topped mountains beyond. To the east and west, the coastline wound its way along in a series of sandy beaches, rocky outcrops and tiny offshore islands, while to the south, the sea – as still as a great turquoise millpond – continued unbroken to the horizon and beyond.

'Doralakia is beautiful, no?' said Konstantin.

'Oh, yes,' said Corby. 'It's the most beautiful town I've ever seen . . .'

'And yet,' said Konstantin, 'I see by your face you are not happy to be here in Doralakia.'

'It's not that,' said Corby, tears springing to her eyes. 'It's just that I'm here by accident. I was travelling on the S.S. *Euphonia* with my family, when I climbed into a crate in the cargo hold—'

'You climbed into a crate?' said the mayor.

'Yes, I was hiding from the clowns.'

'Clowns?' said the mayor.

'Yes, because they'd imprisoned a creature in a wooden box, and it was singing the saddest song.'

'Saddest song?' The mayor was shaking his head now and stroking his long white beard. 'I'm not sure I quite understand, Miss Corby Flood.'

'Well, that's not important right now,' Corby hurried on. 'What *is* important is that when I woke up, I wasn't on board the *Euphonia*. I was in the Hundred-Years-Old Grocery Store and the *Euphonia* was out there, sailing away over the horizon, with my mother and father, and sister and brothers . . .' Tears were flowing freely now, but Corby didn't care. 'And Mama Mesapoliki said that the *Euphonia* wouldn't be back for another year!' she wailed. 'But that you would know what to do . . .'

Konstantin Pavel stopped stroking his long white beard. 'It is true what Mama Mesapoliki says. The *Euphonia* passes Doralakia once a year, but she doesn't stop here . . . Not any more . . .'

KONSTANTIN PAVEL

His face clouded over and he was

silent for a moment. 'Mama Mesapoliki's boys, Spiro and Nico, take their boat and motor out to her, and the captain, he slows down only long enough for them to unload their mama's groceries.'

He smiled kindly, leaning forwards and patting Corby's hand. 'It seems this time, as well as their mama's groceries, Nico and Spiro unloaded you, too. But don't cry, little one. Konstantin Pavel will get you back to your parents and your sister and your brothers . . .'

'You will?' said Corby, wiping her eyes.

'Yes,' said the mayor. 'But first I must know one thing.'

'Yes?' said Corby.

'Why,' said the mayor, 'are you dressed as a bumblebee?'


'But as I told Mr Times-Roman,' said Captain Belvedere gloomily, 'turning back was quite simply out of the question. He and his associates would have to take their complaint to Head Office in Harbour Heights.'

'I blame Arthur,' said Lieutenant Jon-Jolyon

Letchworth-Crisp. 'After all, it's hardly a first officer's job to check the labels on the crates in the cargo hold, now is it?'

'Most unfortunate,' said Captain Belvedere, patting the ship's wheel. 'And just when the *Euphonia* was running so well. Listen to her engine, Lieutenant. It sounds brand new. Why, it takes me back to the *Euphonia*'s maiden voyage with Binky Beiderbecker and Queen Rita—'

'Yes, well, sir. Like I said,' interrupted Jon-Jolyon tetchily, 'the clowns have taken the lifeboat and slipped away into the night, the whole lot of them. The Hattenswillers woke me up this morning to tell me. Couldn't understand a word they were saying, mind you – they had to write it down on funny little notes. Seemed quite upset about the whole thing . . .'

'Dashed poor show, is all I can say,' said Captain Belvedere, shaking his head. 'Still, I'm *not* turning round – missing crate or no missing crate.'

Just then, the door to the bridge flew open and the entire Flood family came crashing in. The entire Flood family, that is, except for Corby.

'Show the captain what you found, boys,' said Mrs Flood, her arms folded.

Toby stepped forward and held out a rusty tin with a faded label on it which read: MULHOLLAND'S CUSTARD AND BANANA PUDDING. Ernest held out a clump of matted straw.

'We found these in the cargo hold,' they announced solemnly.

Captain Belvedere's moustache twitched. 'Just a private business arrangement I have with a little grocery store in Doralakia,' he said. 'It must have

178

fallen out of one of the crates we delivered. I told them to be careful—'

'And this,' Hubert said, holding up a pencil on the end of a piece of string, 'was found next to the tin!'

Mrs Flood gave a little cry. 'Oh no! Tell me it isn't true,' she gasped. 'You delivered my daughter to a little grocery store in Doralakia along with your nasty crates. My poor, dear, darling Corby!'

Serena put an arm round her mother to comfort her, while Jon-Jolyon stepped forward and put an arm round Serena.

'My dear madam, I'm so sorry . . .' began Captain Belvedere, clearly flustered. 'I had no idea—'

'Never mind that, Captain,' said Mr Flood. 'Arthur and I will crank up the engine to full power. There's just one thing I need you to do.'

'Anything,' said Captain Belvedere, gripping the ship's wheel.

'Turn the *Euphonia* round right now!' said Mr Flood. 'And head back to Doralakia!'

'Some more verbena tea?' asked Konstantin. 'Or would you care for another spoonful of that wonderful delicacy you so kindly brought me from the Hundred-Years-Old Grocery Store?'

'No, thank you,' said Corby, wrinkling her nose up at the tin of Snead and Mopwell's Macaroni Cheese in Cheesy Sauce that the mayor was offering to her.

'Here in Doralakia,' Konstantin said, looking at the rusty tin, 'we have olives, sweet cucumbers, honey and wine. But nothing quite like the extraordinary things that are put in tins and delivered to the Hundred-Years-Old Grocery Store! Every tin has a different delicious secret concealed within it!' He laughed delightedly.

The two of them were sitting at the round table, which had a huge lamp on a tall, brass stand in the middle of it, together with a tall teapot, two small teacups, the rusty tin and two long-handled spoons. There was a large full moon in the sky, and all around them lamps shimmered at the top of every tower

house in Doralakia, creating a magical constellation which led down to the pretty harbour below.

'Thank you very much for a delicious tea, Konstantin,' said Corby. 'I've had such a lovely time, but I was wondering . . .'

'How I could help you to get back to your family?' said Konstantin, getting up from the table.

'Yes,' said Corby.

'I shall show you,' said the mayor, hitching up his long white beard and crossing the roof to the tele-scope in the opposite corner.

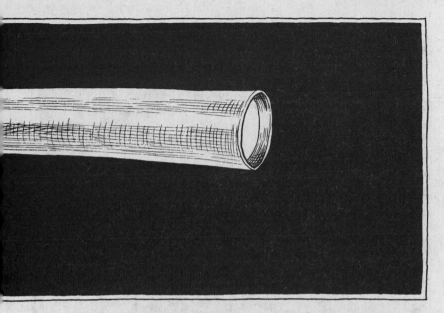

He stepped onto the turntable and swung the telescope round until it was pointing out to sea.
Leaning forward, he peered through the eye-piece,
and began twiddling with several small wheels until
the telescope was focused on the distant horizon.
Then he beckoned for Corby to take a look.

Corby put her eye to the telescope.

And there, far out on the glittering sea,
surrounded by shimmering shoals of love fish, and
lit up with countless lights, was a magnificent
ocean liner. It reminded Corby of the faded poster

of the *Euphonia* in her glory days that she loved so much.

'The *Queen Rita the Second*,' said Konstantin. 'She is far too grand for any of our little harbours here in Dalcretia. No, she sails the seven seas on marvellous cruises to faraway places. But she does do us the honour of slowing down, so that her passengers can enjoy the lights of Fedrun and Mesapoli, Lissari, and of course Doralakia, glittering in the distance by night – and watch the spectacular sunrise over our tower houses the next day.'

'She's beautiful,' breathed Corby, unable to tear herself away.

'You think so?' said Konstantin, a tinge of sadness in his voice. 'As for me, the *Euphonia* will always be first in my heart . . .'

He seemed lost in thought for a moment, then pulled himself together.

'Tomorrow, at first light, Nico and Spiro can take you out to the *Queen Rita the Second* in their boat. I shall give you thirty gold Dalcretian crowns for the finest cabin, and you, my dear Corby Flood, shall reach Harbour Heights a full day before your

185

family. Think how surprised they'll be!' The mayor clapped his hands together.

'But how will I be able to repay you?' said Corby excitedly.

'You shall repay me by always thinking fondly of Doralakia and' – he took Corby's hand and helped her down from the telescope – 'by coming back one day to visit our little town.'

Just then, there was the sound of a bell tinkling nearby.

'Please excuse me,' said Konstantin as he crossed the terrace to a copper and silver tube – just like the one Corby had seen next to the door downstairs – protruding from the wall. Konstantin removed a cork stopper and spoke into the funnel.

'Hello?'

The terrace filled with the sound of two voices, both shouting, both interrupting one another in the language Corby couldn't understand. She recognized them at once. It was Nico and Spiro.

'OK. OK,' she heard Konstantin say. He turned to Corby, a look of bemusement on his face. 'The strangest thing,' he said. 'Nico and Spiro. They say

their mama has found a soulopol in the Hundred-Years-Old Grocery Store, and this time it isn't a little girl dressed up as a bumblebee . . .'

'It isn't?' said Corby.

'No,' said Konstantin. 'Come quick, they say, because this time the soulopol – it is real!'

# 16. The Soulopol

*Someone has come. But it is not the little girl, it is an old woman with a huge black head. I'm frightened. What part of the forest is this? It smells strange and it makes my nose itch . . .*

*I'm . . . going . . . to . . . sneeze . . .*

'Atishoo! Atishoo! Atishoo!'

The sound of sneezing was coming from the Hundred-Years-Old Grocery Store, and with each sneeze, the crowd of Doralakians in nightgowns and pyjamas drew back and chattered nervously to each other in the language Corby didn't understand.

'The people of Doralakia, they go to bed very early,' explained Konstantin as they hurried down the steep cobbled street towards the grocery store. 'Doralakia has become a very sleepy little town ever since the laughing goat, she . . .'

Konstantin's voice trailed off as they reached the crowd.

Nico and Spiro, in matching nightshirts covered in patches, stood at the front of the throng of townspeople, the tassels of their red caps dancing about as they talked animatedly. Spiro held a large frying pan in his hand, while Nico clutched a heavy rolling pin. Between them, Mama Mesapoliki chattered away in a high-pitched, squeaky voice and waved her broomstick about, as if to emphasize what she was saying. Around her, the townsfolk exchanged nervous looks.

'Mama, she say the soulopol is in a box that came from the ship,' said Nico.

'She say the soulopol follow the little bumblebee here to our grocery store,' continued Spiro. 'Is not good to wear wings and stripy-stripy body, Mama say, because soulopol, they think you make fun of them!'

All eyes turned to Corby, who suddenly felt her face flush red.

'*Atishoo!*'

The crowd gasped and drew back. Mama Mesapoliki brandished

her broomstick and muttered under her breath.

'Mama, she say,' said Nico and Spiro together, 'the soulopol, it angry!'

'*Atishoo! Atishoo! Atishoo!*'

All of a sudden there was a loud crash, and a tumble of tin cans cascaded out of the half-open door of the

Hundred-Years-Old Grocery Store and down the steps onto the cobbled street.

'Mama's pyramid of tins!' cried Spiro and Nico.

Konstantin shook his head. 'First the laughing goat and now a haunted grocery store. Poor Doralakia! Who would want to visit us now when they hear that we have a soulopol!'

Corby stamped her foot. 'What nonsense!' she said. 'I'm just a little girl in a fancy dress costume, and *I* know that it isn't a soulopol in there.' She bent down and picked up a tin can.

'It isn't?' said Konstantin.

'No,' said Corby. 'And what's more, I'm going to prove it.'

She pushed past the astonished onlookers and strode up the steps to the front door of the grocery store.

'Do you need my frying pan?' asked Nico helpfully.

'Or my rolling pin?' offered Spiro.

Mama Mesapoliki held out her broom. 'Bumblebee?' she said kindly.

Corby shook her head and looked down at the rusty tin can in her hand.

'No, thank you,' she said. 'But there is one thing I *do* need.'

'What?' asked Konstantin, hitching his beard over his shoulder. 'A sword? A shotgun? A magic spell?'

'No,' said Corby. 'A tin opener.'

# 17. The Hundred-Year-Old Pineapple Chunks

*he falling rocks have stopped and the dust has settled, but I am still trapped in here in this hollow tree, no matter how much I stamp my feet and push against the trunk. But wait! Someone is coming . . .*

Corby pushed open the door and stepped into the grocery store. The floor was strewn with tin cans, and on the counter only the first two rows of Mama Mesapoliki's tin-can pyramid remained. Beneath the huge scales, which were now at a jaunty angle, was a jumble of wooden crates from the S.S. *Euphonia*. The one at the bottom had shifted and knocked over the others piled on top of it. A large, doleful eye peered out from between its wooden slats.

Corby opened her *Hoffendinck's Guide* and turned

to the page with the label.

This was all her fault. If she had left the label on the crate, then Nico and Spiro wouldn't have thought it was meant for their mama's grocery store and unloaded it. She read the name on the label.

'Mr Times-Roman,' she said. Perhaps it was just as well the crate wasn't still on board after all.

Corby approached slowly, the open tin of Happy Island Pineapple Chunks in Syrup in one hand and Konstantin's penknife, with its tin-opening attachment, in the other. The large, doleful eye watched her.

She bent down, reached into the tin and drew out a glistening pineapple chunk, which she gently pushed through the slats in the crate. There was a snuffling and then a slurping sound.

'There, there,' Corby whispered soothingly. 'You poor thing. It's high time someone got you out of that nasty crate, whatever you are.'

And that someone, Corby realized, taking a deep breath, would have to be her.

She looked at Konstantin's penknife and then at the wooden slats. Like the bars of a cage, they had been hammered into place with nails at regular intervals. It occurred to her that if she used the penknife, then she could prise the nails out of the wood, one by one, and free the creature. It would take quite a while, but in the meantime, there were plenty of pineapple chunks left.

'Mama say, what take Corby Bumblebee so long?' whispered Nico to the mayor. 'Has the soulopol cast a spell on her?'

They were all sitting on the steps of the Hundred-Years-Old Grocery Store: Nico, Spiro, Mama Mesapoliki, Konstantin Pavel, and Yanni Fulda, the clockmaker, and his pretty daughter Lara, who lived in the tower house next door and were the only other townsfolk who hadn't gone back to bed. The moon was low in the sky and dawn was beginning to break over the mountains.

'For the last time,' said Konstantin, 'Corby says it isn't a soulopol. You heard her. And she said we must keep very quiet.'

'But that was two hours ago,' protested Spiro, 'and if she doesn't come

out of Mama's store soon, she'll miss the big ship.'

He pointed across the harbour to where, far out at sea, the lights of the majestic *Queen Rita II* had just appeared in the distance.

Lara, the clockmaker's daughter, gave a little sigh. 'The big ship,' she murmured.

Just then, Corby stuck her head round the door. She looked tired, and her hair had bits of straw in it.

'*Ssshhh*,' she said. 'All of you. You'll scare it. I've just got it settled.'

'The soulopol?' said Nico.

Konstantin gave him a look.

'Come and see for yourself,' said Corby, 'but you must keep very quiet. The poor thing has been shut up in that horrid crate for ages, and it's terribly frightened.'

Nico and Spiro bent down and whispered in their mother's ear. Then they all followed Corby inside the grocery store, closing the door quietly behind them.

'It's magnificent!' said Nico.

'Astonishing!' whispered Spiro. 'Mama say, she seen nothing like it, and Mama, she born in Mesapoli!'

'Beautiful!' breathed Lara, the clockmaker's daughter.

'If I hadn't heard it with my own ears I wouldn't have believed it,' added her father.

'Doralakia is blessed to have such a creature!' beamed Mayor Konstantin Pavel. 'Why, the laughing goat was truly remarkable, but this . . . this . . .' He clasped his hands together and tears sprang to his eyes. 'This will put Doralakia back on the map . . . We shall take such care of it, Corby Flood, I promise you.'

'Just until I get back to Harbour Heights and speak to my father,' said Corby. 'He'll know what to do.'

'Speaking of which,' said the mayor, 'you must hurry if you are not to miss the *Queen Rita*.'

They turned and quietly tiptoed out of the Hundred-Years-Old Grocery Store.

Behind them, from the nest of straw in the corner, piled high and with the tin cans removed, came a contented sigh.

# 18. The Sweetest Song

 *t is so nice here in the fresh dry grass. The little girl freed me from the hollow tree. Others came, too. I sang, and they smiled and laughed and stroked my skin.*

*And now the sun has come up. I am so happy, my heart will burst! I must sing again. If I sing, I can let the happiness out and my heart will not burst . . .*

Down at the pretty harbourside of Doralakia, Corby climbed into Nico and Spiro's boat. It had a rickety old engine strapped to its wooden hull, which was light blue, and had an eye painted on the prow.

'To see where she going,' Nico explained, making sure Corby was settled on a bench before he started the engine, by pulling a long cord.

The old engine spluttered into life after two more pulls.

'Farewell, Corby Flood,' called Konstantin Pavel, waving his handkerchief. 'And may St George protect and watch over you. I only wish you could stay, for today Doralakia shall have its Longest Afternoon and the people shall see the marvellous creature you have entrusted to our care.'

'Goodbye, Konstantin!' called Corby. 'Goodbye, Mama Mesapoliki. Goodbye, Doralakia! I'm sorry

I can't stay for the Longest Afternoon . . .'

Spiro lowered the engine into the water and the
light-blue boat surged out into the harbour at quite
a surprising speed. Corby waved to the figures,
rapidly receding into the distance on the harbour
quayside, the tower houses rising up behind them like
golden stalagmites in the early morning sunshine.

She turned away, and felt a lump in her throat.
Looking down, she weighed the small leather bag she
held in her hand. The thirty Dalcretian crowns

Konstantin had given her jingled inside.

After about fifteen minutes the huge hull of the gleaming ocean liner drew closer, and Corby could see its decks, which were strewn with streamers and balloons and long lengths of glittering tinsel.

The Halfway-There Ceremony on the *Queen Rita II* looked as if it had been far more fun than the one on the S.S. *Euphonia*, thought Corby. It seemed so long ago – the party games, the food fight, Serena and Arthur, Serena and Jon-Jolyon, the sinister Brotherhood of Clowns . . .

Corby shivered.

'You cold, Corby Bumblebee?' asked Nico. 'We nearly there, but you can have my jacket. Finest goatskin . . .'

'No, it's all right,' said Corby, turning back and smiling at him.

And then she saw it . . . over Nico's left shoulder, a white lifeboat, far in the distance.

It was being rowed steadily towards a deserted sandy cove. And as she watched, four figures clambered out into the surf and hauled the lifeboat ashore as a fifth figure waved his hands in the air – and then his legs, as he fell over in the back of the boat.

But it wasn't this that had first caught Corby's eye, nor the fact that the lifeboat looked curiously familiar. No, what Corby had noticed, even at this distance, was a flash of colour that chilled her to the bone.

The figures, who had pulled the boat ashore and were now heading off across the beach, were wearing bottle-green bowler hats!

'For the last time,' said Yanni Fulda, the clockmaker, 'come away, Lara, and stop mooning after the big ship.'

'But Papa!' protested Lara. 'You don't understand!'

Next to them, the mayor wiped his eyes and blew his nose loudly on his handkerchief. He turned away from the harbour, and was about to climb the steep, cobbled street back to his tower house, when the most extraordinary sound floated through the still early-morning air.

It was a sweet, lilting sound, like a songbird greeting the dawn, or a whale calling to its calf – and it was coming from the Hundred-Years-Old Grocery Store. It was the sweetest song Konstantin Pavel had ever heard. All through Doralakia, the townspeople were throwing open the shutters of their tower-house windows and peering out.

Konstantin laughed and began to walk up the street, and as he did so, he called up to the people: 'Today, Doralakia shall have the Longest Afternoon! Spread the word!' he called. 'The Longest Afternoon ever!'

'What do you mean *turn round*, Corby Bumblebee?' said Spiro incredulously.

'But we almost at the big ship!' protested Nico.

'I know, I know,' said Corby, clutching *Hoffendinck's*

*Guide* more tightly than ever. 'But the Brotherhood of Clowns! They've come back! We must warn the mayor!'

'And what about your family?' said Spiro.

'Your mother, your father, your sister and your brothers?' said Nico.

'I know, I know,' said Corby, tears streaming down her face. It was the most difficult decision she had ever had to make, but she knew she couldn't board the *Queen Rita II* and simply sail away, not with the Brotherhood of Clowns on the loose. 'Turn round!' she sobbed. 'Just turn round!'

Spiro shook his head, and Nico muttered in the

language that Corby didn't understand, but they turned the boat in a wide arc and, as the great ocean liner glided past, headed back to Doralakia.

It was then that it happened.

The rickety old engine gave a wheezy, choking, rattling cough and spluttered to a stop. The boat began to drift out to sea.

'What now?' said Corby, trying to sound calmer than she felt.

Nico and Spiro produced two small paddles.

'We sail, how you say . . .'

'Under our own steam,' said Spiro.

'Only,' added Nico, 'it might take rather a long time!'

# 19. The Longest Afternoon

 *have been bathed and my skin has been oiled. I am wearing garlands of sweet-smelling flowers. It is almost as if I was back in the palace gardens, only better . . .*

*But what is this? A sweet white petal? Where did that come from?*

*It tastes good . . . Look, there is another . . . And another . . .*

*Mmmm!*

Doralakia looked spectacular. All morning the towns-folk had worked feverishly, making the garlands of flowers and preparing the brightly coloured banners that now festooned every tower house.

They had strung rows of paper lanterns on ropes between the tall walls of the buildings, and set out

ESPADORIOTS

long tables round the harbourside, which they were now piling high with all the delicious food that Doralakia had to offer. Strings of spicy sausages and great jars of juicy olives nestled between huge platters, piled high with honeyed pancakes and sweet cucumbers. Flat, oven-fresh bread filled the harbour air with a delicious aroma, as did the huge dishes of espadoriots – rich custard flans for which Dalcretia was rightly famous.

In pride of place was the table outside the Hundred-Years-Old Grocery Store, on which Mama Mesapoliki had laid out her most treasured tins: AMBERSIDE'S STEWED PRUNES; TARTAN BOB'S CORNED BEEF HASH WITH ONIONS. And the magnificent corrugated-

AMBERSIDE'S STEWED PRUNES

sided square-shaped tin with two keys stuck to its lid – ARCHDUKE FERDINAND'S SARDINES ON BUTTERED TOAST, WITH EXTRA TOAST!

The front of the Hundred-Years-Old Grocery Store was bedecked with garlands of flowers from the mountain meadows, and a wooden ramp covered in red carpet had been placed at its front steps. Outside, the Doralakia town band – in freshly laundered red caps with tassels on the ends – were tuning up their eighteen-string baloukies – large stringed instruments, made of brass, that could be played with a bow and blown into at the same time.

Everywhere, people were talking and singing, dancing and clapping, laughing and exchanging excited greetings. Not just the townsfolk of Doralakia either,

211

for news had spread fast along the
Dalcretian coast that today
Doralakia was to have a
Longest Afternoon.
All morning, small
parties had been arriving from
Fedrun, Lissari and even
Mesapoli, bearing gifts
and contributions
for the festivities.
There were fish-
ermen wearing tall
fedrun hats carrying jars of honey,
Lissari matrons in colourful
turbans bringing fabric banners,
and a party of five old ladies in
the black cloaks, long dresses
and large turbans of Mesapoli,
carrying an enormous rolled-up
carpet. They seemed to be in
rather a bad mood, so nobody
paid them much attention.

The streets and tower houses of

Doralakia buzzed with rumours and gossip about the extraordinary creature in the grocery store. Some said it was a sneezing bear, others that it was a reciting dog, while others were utterly convinced that a laughing goat had returned to Doralakia.

But whatever the truth or otherwise of these rumours, one thing was certain. Neither Mayor Pavel nor Mama Mesapoliki was saying a word, and nor was the clockmaker or his beautiful daughter, Lara.

And as for Spiro and Nico Mesapoliki, well, nobody had clapped eyes on them since they'd taken the little girl in the bumblebee costume to catch the big ship.

'Wait till twelve o'clock,' was all Mayor Pavel would say with a huge smile and a wag of his long white beard, when anyone asked him. 'But one thing I *will* tell you is that you won't be disappointed!'

The sun was high in the sky by the time the pale-blue boat finally reached the shore. Despite Spiro and Nico paddling furiously, the strong Dalcretian tides had swept them down the coast, far from Doralakia.

'At last,' gasped Spiro, pulling the boat onto the pebbly beach. 'On land we will make fast time, Corby Flood.'

'Now we travel as the goat gallops,' said Nico, stooping down so that Corby could climb onto his shoulders. 'Up and over the mountains to Doralakia. Spiro, he know the short cut.'

They set off, leaping from boulder to boulder as they scaled the mountainside in front of them. Corby looked back. Nico was right, they *were* travelling fast. Already the beach was far behind them, and in a few

minutes they were almost at the top of the mountain. As they came over the peak, the bleats of the mountain goats filling the air all round them, Corby saw the tower houses of Doralakia in the distance.

Down the mountain they ran – as sure-footed as the mountain goats – and up the other side. Half an hour later Corby could see, not only the tops of the tower houses, but also the streets between them and the pretty harbourside, thronging with the colourful crowds who had gathered for the Longest Afternoon.

'Not long now,' panted Spiro.

'Almost there,' gasped Nico.

'Watch out!' cried Corby.

For there, in the middle of the rocky goat track, sat five little old ladies in yellowing underwear, their arms tied firmly behind their backs.

'Aunties!' shouted Nico and Spiro, coming to an abrupt halt. 'Where are your black cloaks, your long dresses, your large turbans . . . ?'

Twelve o'clock arrived and the big crowd in the pretty harbour square could scarcely contain their excitement. Mayor Pavel raised his hand and the Doralakia

town band broke into a spirited rendition of 'The Lament of St George'. As it finished, Mama Mesapoliki opened the door of the Hundred-Years-

Old Grocery Store and the crowd waited . . .

And waited . . .

And waited . . .

A low buzz spread through the crowd. Where was the amazing creature? Mayor Pavel and Mama Mesapoliki exchanged puzzled glances and disappeared inside the grocery store. Moments later, they emerged.

'Mama Mesapoliki, she say,' gasped Mayor Pavel, 'that the back door is wide open. And the creature, it has disappeared!'

Just then, there came a chorus of indignant shrieks as a bunch of tiny old ladies in yellowed underwear came rushing down the steep, cobbled streets, shouting at the tops of their voices, together with Spiro and Nico, who had Corby Flood up on his shoulders.

'Mama's sisters from Mesapoli,' shouted Nico. 'They say five men in green hats the colour of bottles, they stole their clothes and their second-best picnic carpet!'

'Look!' shouted Corby, pointing. 'Over there!'

The crowd turned and there, down by the harbour

quayside, were the five old ladies in black cloaks who everyone had assumed were from Mesapoli. They were sneaking out of town, clutching an enormous rolled-up carpet. The crowd looked at the tiny old ladies in their underwear who had surrounded Mama Mesapoliki, and were waving their arms about like tiny windmills, then back at the old ladies at the harbourside. The puzzled murmurs grew louder.

'Don't just stand there!' cried Corby helplessly, as Nico and Spiro tried to barge their way through the crowd. 'Somebody . . . *any*body! *Do something!*'

As the last of the cloaked old ladies disappeared round the corner of the quayside square, the crowd surged forwards, pointing and shouting and waving their hands in the air. Up the steep cobbled Street of Hatmakers they ran, through Fishwife Square and down Laughing Goat Lane, chasing after the old ladies – who seemed remarkably quick and strong for their age. Then, as they rounded the water pump at the end of the Avenue of Tassel Weavers, the crowd came to a stumbling halt.

Up on Nico's shoulders, Corby looked round desperately. Which way had they gone? She didn't know – and neither, it seemed, did the crowd, who were all pointing this way and that and scratching their heads.

Just then, from the top of the tallest tower house in Doralakia, a familiar voice rang out.

'The mayor,' said Spiro excitedly to Corby, 'he say, they went that way!'

'Back to our pretty harbour,' said Nico.

The crowd surged back down the hill and, sure enough, there at the quayside once more were the old ladies – four of them still clutching the rolled-up carpet, while the fifth struggled to untie a gently bobbing fishing boat.

'Stop them!' Corby shouted. 'They're getting away!'

As the crowd closed in, one of the old ladies slipped and bumped into another, who slipped and bumped into the next, who slipped and bumped into the next.

All four old ladies fell over and lay there, waggling their feet in the air.

Somebody in the crowd giggled. Then somebody else, and then, like a wave breaking on the harbour quayside, the whole crowd burst into laughter.

The fifth old lady spun round and tore off her cloak.

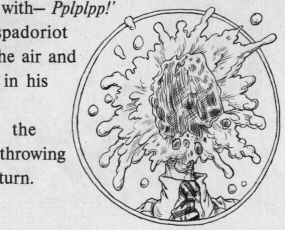

'Mr Times-Roman!' shouted Corby above the laughter of the crowd.

'Nobody laughs at the Brotherhood of Clowns!' snarled Mr Times-Roman, shaking his fist. 'And gets away with— *Pplplpp!*'

A custard espadoriot sailed through the air and landed squarely in his face.

'Oi!' shouted the second old lady, throwing off his cloak in turn.

*Splat!*

222

Mr Franklin-Gothic, too, received a face full of Dalcretian custard flan, and the crowd roared with laughter all the louder.

*Splat! Splat! Splat!*

Mr Bembo, Mr Palatino and Mr Garamond all got a face full. They tripped over the enormous carpet and fell into the harbour, taking a wildly flailing Franklin-Gothic and Times-Roman with them.

The crowd broke into loud applause. Moving out from behind a quayside table piled high with espadoriot flans, four boys stepped forward and took a bow.

'Cedric! Hubert! Ernest! Toby!' Corby cried, as Nico reached the front of the crowd and helped her down from his shoulders.

'Those naughty clowns,' said Spiro, beside him.

'We help them out of the water,' said Nico, 'then Mama, she have a very stern word with them!'

'Hi, sis!' cried Toby, giving her a hug. 'Thought you looked as if you needed a hand.'

'Well played!' laughed Ernest.

'Nicely done!' agreed Hubert.

'Crisp as a Gibbons shirt on washday,' added Cedric.

Corby gave each of them an enormous hug.

'And Mother and Father?' she asked. 'And Serena?'

'They're right behind us,' said Toby, pointing out to sea. 'Father said we could come on ahead in one of the lifeboats he's modified. They're brilliant!'

Around her, the crowd had broken into wild cheering as the deep sound of a ship's horn rang out. Corby turned and there, coming into the harbour of the little town of Doralakia for the first time in so, so long, was none other than the S.S. *Euphonia* herself!

# 20. Mr. Hoffendinck

*here am I? It's dark . . .*
     *I can hear laughter . . . clapping . . .*
*cheers . . .*

The S.S. *Euphonia* docked at the harbour quayside in moments, and a gangplank descended smoothly on perfectly functioning mechanical arms. The crowd cheered and threw their red tasselled caps high in the air as the Doralakia town band struck up 'The Lament of St George', which was the only tune they all knew.

Mr and Mrs Flood waved to the crowd as they came ashore, followed by Serena and a shifty-looking Lieutenant Jon-Jolyon Letchworth-Crisp.

'Darling!' exclaimed Mrs Flood, rushing up and hugging her youngest child. 'We were so worried!'

Mr Flood took off his glasses and seemed to have something in his eye. 'Daughter!' he said, and knelt down and embraced Corby.

'Father!' Corby cried. 'I tried to tell you about the creature but—'

'Jonny!' came a loud shriek, and Lara, the clockmaker's beautiful daughter, came rushing through the crowd. 'Jon-Jonny! Is you! From the big ship!' She clasped Lieutenant Jon-Jolyon Letchworth-Crisp in a big hug.

Jon-Jolyon looked distinctly uncomfortable. 'Ah, Serena,' he said, as smoothly as he could manage. 'Let me introduce you to Lara Fulda. I made her father's acquaintance a few years ago, when I was . . . er . . . fourth engineer aboard the *Queen Rita* . . .'

'The big ship!' said Lara. 'But Jon-Jonny, why you so cold? And why you no come back? You said you loved me, remember, Jonny?'

'Please, Serena,' said Jon-Jolyon, trying to prise Lara off. 'Let me explain—'

*Thwack!*

Serena slapped his face, then marched over to a smiling Corby and hugged her.

'Lara, please, I—' began Jon-Jolyon.

*Thwack!*

Lara turned and marched off towards her father's tower house.

Just then, Arthur appeared at the top of the gangplank. He was standing next to the man from Cabin 21, and he had his arm around his shoulders. He seemed to be coaxing him to step onto the gangplank, though without much success.

'Come on, Father,' Arthur was saying. 'It's been so long since you last set foot on dry land . . .'

'Father?' said Serena, turning and running back up

227

the gangplank. 'I had no idea that you were Arthur's father,' she said.

'Yes,' said Arthur, a little sadly, Corby thought. 'Father is the reason I cannot leave the *Euphonia*.'

Serena turned to Arthur's father and smiled sweetly. 'Come on,' she said. 'Take my hand. It'll be all right, trust me.'

The man from Cabin 21 trembled, but put a foot tentatively on the gangplank all the same.

'That's the way,' smiled Serena. 'You can do it.'

Slowly and unsteadily, the man from Cabin 21 crept down the gangplank and, pausing for an instant, stepped onto the quayside of Doralakia.

'My old friend!' cried Mayor Konstantin Pavel, rushing up and falling to his knees. 'How can you ever forgive me and Doralakia for your terrible loss?'

The man from Cabin 21 took off his dark glasses with trembling fingers and looked deep into Mayor Konstantin's eyes.

'It's been too long, Konstantin,' he said in a shaky voice. 'All those years I shut myself away with my memories . . .' He looked at Arthur and Serena, who were holding hands, and back at the mayor. 'The time

has come to move on,' he said. 'Of course I forgive you, old friend.'

Just then, Konstantin saw Corby, and he motioned her to join him. 'I have someone here I'd like you to meet,' he said. 'Corby Flood, this is Mr Hoffendinck.' And he smiled at the look of surprise on Corby's face.

'Very pleased to meet you, Corby Flood,' said Mr Hoffendinck. 'Very pleased indeed.'

For a minute, Corby was lost for words. Then, her fingers trembling, she held out her copy of *Hoffendinck's Guide*. 'I've read every word,' she breathed.

At that moment Mr and Mrs Hattenswiller appeared together with Captain Boris Belvedere who, for once, wasn't looking his usual gloomy self. Instead, he had a twinkle in his eye and a positively jaunty spring in his step as he walked down the gang-plank.

'Ah, there you are, little girl!' he smiled, twitching his walrus moustache. 'The Hattenswillers here are full of admiration for your courage and quick-wittedness.'

'They are?' said Corby.

'Whiffl-whhiffl!' said Mrs Hattenswiller.

'Mmumm-mmumm!' said Mr Hattenswiller.

'You see!' said Captain Belvedere delightedly. 'The Hattenswillers are world-famous private detectives. They specialize in clown crime and have been on the trail of the Brotherhood of Clowns for months.'

'You mean, you can actually understand what they're saying?' said Corby, amazed.

'But of course, clear as a bell,' said Captain Belvedere with a dry laugh. It was the first time Corby had heard him laugh. 'They heard of the theft of the personal property of the Begum of Dandoon.

231

Snatched from the palace gardens, they tell me. They recognized it as the work of the brotherhood straight away. They were planning to spring their trap when we got to Harbour Heights, but that was before the Brotherhood of Clowns ran into *you* . . .'

'Mmumm-mmm,' said Mr Hattenswiller, nodding his conical hat at Corby.

'Precisely,' said Captain Belvedere with another dry laugh. 'Very well put, Hattenswiller, old chap. Anyway, you – my dear little girl – have caught them red-handed! I wouldn't be surprised if there wasn't a substantial reward, knowing the Begum!'

But Corby wasn't listening, because she'd heard a sound. It was like a sad wolf singing to the moon, or a lonely songbird calling to its mate . . . And it was coming from the enormous rolled-up carpet on the quayside.

Corby rushed over to it, followed by the mayor, Mr Hoffendinck, her parents, her brothers, Captain Belvedere, the Hattenswillers, Arthur and Serena, Lieutenant Jon-Jolyon Letchworth-Crisp, who was ruefully rubbing two very red cheeks, Mama Mesapoliki, her sisters, and Spiro and Nico with five very wet clowns in their clutches.

'Stand back, everyone!' commanded Mayor Konstantin Pavel. 'The Longest Afternoon is about to commence,' he announced, as Corby leaned down and gently unrolled the carpet . . .

# Epilogue

# THE TOWNS OF THE DALCRETIAN COAST

## DORALAKIA

The highlight of any cruise along the Dalcretian coast is a visit to the little town of Doralakia, hidden jewel of Dalcretia. Situated on the very tip of the Dalcretian peninsula, the lights from its extraordinary tower houses are a truly magical sight when seen from the sea.

The Doralakians are amongst the friendliest and most hospitable of all the Dalcretians, and taking tea in a tower house as the moon rises is an experience never forgotten. The harbourside is well worth a visit, as is the famous Hundred-Years-Old Grocery Store, with its fascinating collection of antique canned goods.

But the highlight of any visit to Doralakia must be the Longest Afternoon, at which the remarkable singing rhinoceros is sure to make an appearance. The Emerald rhinoceros of the Dandoon Delta was rescued by the Doralakians and later formally presented to the town by the Begum of Dandoon, who recognized how happy it was in its new home. She and her granddaughter visit it each year.

THE EMERALD RHINOCEROS

# NOTES

# From a quayside wall near Cyclops Point:

## THE S.S. EUPHONIA

### Empress of the Seas

**ENJOY** the voyage of a lifetime aboard this recently
fully restored miracle of nautical engineering!

**CRUISE** the oceans of the world and explore
the magical places along the way!

**BOOK NOW** for the deluxe ten-ports-of-call
cruise and receive your free copy of the famous
*Hoffendinck's Guide* (revised edition).

*Hoffendinck, Belvedere and Flood,*
*Quality Cruise Ships Ltd*

From the *Montmorency Gazette*:

# Montmorency Gazette

## CLOWN CRIME IS NO LAUGHING MATTER

*(From our crime correspondent)*

MISS LUCIDA BLACKLETTER

Today, the Harbour police announced the arrest of Lucida Blackletter, B.F., A.C., M.M., O.L.S.C., D.D.D., headmistress of Harbour Heights School, in a spectacular sting operation. Lying in wait in a large wooden crate, officers pounced when Miss Blackletter visited the Harbour warehouse to claim her goods.

Miss Blackletter, a renowned collector of handmade shoes and exotic handbags, is charged with masterminding the abduction and smuggling of an Emerald rhinoceros from the palace gardens of the Begum of Dandoon by the Brotherhood of Clowns, the notorious clown gang currently awaiting trial. She planned to turn the creature into handmade shoes and exotic handbags when it was fully grown.

Miss Blackletter has refused to comment, but Chief Inspector Wilsden Marchmain said, 'Clown crime is no laughing matter.'

# Marriage Announcements:

- *Announcement* -

MR & MRS WINTHROP FLOOD ARE PROUD TO ANNOUNCE

THE FORTHCOMING MARRIAGE OF THEIR DAUGHTER SERENA,

TO ARTHUR, SON OF MR HOFFENDINCK,

AT A CEREMONY TO TAKE PLACE AT THE CYCLOPS POINT LIGHTHOUSE,

CAPTAIN BORIS BELVEDERE OFFICIATING,

FOLLOWED BY A SUNSET CRUISE ON BOARD THE S.S. *EUPHONIA*

# PΣOPLΣ OF DORΔLΔKIΔ!

LARA FULDA, THE CLOCKMAKER'S

DAUGHTER, IS TO MARRY

JON-JOLYON LETCHWORTH-CRISP,

OF THE BIG SHIP, NEXT WEEK,

FOLLOWED BY THE LONGEST AFTERNOON

DANCING TILL DAWN - NO GOATS

ON THE ROOFTOPS!

BY ORDER OF KONSTANTIN PAVEL, MAYOR

From the *Scowling Mermaid*, school magazine
of the school ship *Betty-Jeanne*:

THE
SCOWLING MERMAID
SUMMER TERM

SCHOOL MAGAZINE OF THE SCHOOL SHIP *BETTY-JEANNE*
EDITOR: FERGUS CRANE

NEW PUPILS JOIN OUR SCHOOL
The Scowling Mermaid is pleased to announce
the arrival of five new pupils at the school
ship *Betty-Jeanne*. The Flood children, Cedric,
Hubert, Ernest, Toby and Corby, join us from
the Dandoon Delta, where their father was
recently bridge building.

The boys are keen to organize a deck sports
team for next season. (See the school notice
board.)

HARBOUR HEIGHTS SCHOOL TO CLOSE
The school ship can expect plenty more new
pupils as Harbour Heights has announced that

And a cable which arrived this morning:

TO MISS CORBY FLOOD . . .STOP

. . .CLOWNS HAVE ESCAPED . . .

STOP . . .NEED YOUR HELP . . .

STOP . . .COME STRAIGHT AWAY

. . .STOP . . .MR & MRS HATTENSWILLER

PAUL STEWART

PAUL STEWART is a highly regarded author of books for young readers—everything from picture books to football stories, fantasy, and horror. Several of his books are published by Random House Children's Books, including *The Wakening,* which was selected as a Pick of the Year by the Federation of Children's Book Groups.

Together with Chris Riddell, he is co-creator of the Edge Chronicles series, which has sold over two million books and is now available in over thirty languages; the Barnaby Grimes series; and two more books in the Far-Flung Adventures series: *Fergus Crane,* which won a Smarties Prize Gold Medal, and *Hugo Pepper.*

CHRIS RIDDELL is an accomplished graphic artist who has illustrated many acclaimed books for children, including *Pirate Diary* by Richard Platt and *Gulliver,* which both won the Kate Greenaway Medal. *Something Else* by Kathryn Cave was short-listed and *Castle Diary* by Richard Platt was Highly Commended for the Kate Greenaway Medal.

Together with Paul Stewart, he is co-creator of the Edge Chronicles series, which has sold over two million books and is now available in over thirty languages; the Barnaby Grimes series; and two more books in the Far-Flung Adventures series: *Fergus Crane,* which won a Smarties Prize Gold Medal, and *Hugo Pepper.*

EMIL HOFFENDINCK

EMIL HOFFENDINCK, writer, explorer and
bibliophile, is the author of the acclaimed
*Hoffendinck's Guide*, for many years the essential
companion for any sea-faring traveller. Now in its new
revised edition, *Hoffendinck's Guide* is once again
available to all travellers in search of the overlooked,
the undervisited or the misunderstood.